Hope

Sow Seeds of

To Sis. Barb
Happy Birthday!
Love,
Sis. Daire

Other Books by MARY WALLACE

Broken Dragon
Caribbean Call
Center of Interest
Curtain of Time
Elly
God Answers Prayer
He Stands Tall
It's Real
Light for Living
Moving On
My Name Is Christian Woman
Old-Time Preacher Men
Pioneer Pentecostal Women, Vol. I-III
Profiles of Pentecostal Missionaries
Profiles of Pentecostal Preachers, Vol. I-II

Dr. Carter
Garneau
Prof Cen
1:50
May 10th
ENT Specialist

Ashley

Sow Seeds of Hope

MARY WALLACE

WORD AFLAME PRESS

Sow Seeds of Hope

by Mary Wallace

© 2004, Word Aflame Press
Hazelwood, MO 63042-2299

Cover Design by Shane Long

Printed in United States of America

Printed by

WORD AFLAME PRESS
8855 Dunn Road, Hazelwood, MO 63042
www.pentecostalpublishing.com

Library of Congress Cataloging-in-Publication Data

Wallace, Mary H.
    Sow seeds of hope / by Mary H. Wallace.
        p. cm.
    Includes bibliographical references (p.).
    ISBN 1-56722-653-1
    1. Hope—Religious aspects—Christianity. I. Title.

    BV4638.W35 2004
    234'.25—dc22

                                     2004054995

Contents

Preface

More than twelve years ago while I was still editor of the Pentecostal Publishing House, I felt led to write a book on faith, hope, and charity. I began collecting books on those subjects. In 1992 my husband, J. O., and I left the Pentecostal Publishing House and retired to a farm in Columbus, Mississippi, where I opened a small Christian bookstore.

At first I focused on finishing our family biography, which was published that year. Then I helped Brother and Sister Robert Arthur write their biography, *Broken Dragon*. Later I hit sort of a dry spell with writing and turned my interest to my little bookstore while still adding to my collection of studies on faith, hope, and charity.

After a few years in Mississippi, we moved back to our hometown of Nashville. After getting settled here, I began to think again about writing. "How about a devotional?" I wondered. "I used to write those for the adult Sunday school curriculum." So I began, slowly writing two or three. Sometimes one every day.

We attended First Pentecostal Church in West Nashville, where Brother Ron Becton is pastor. Brother Becton's preaching style is somewhat like his father's, Brother C. M. Becton—very focused, a clear-cut subject then several good illustrations. I found my notes on several of his sermons. They translated easily into devotional style, so by the end of 2000, I had finished my book.

"I have probably lost my readers," I worried as I sent the manuscript to Morris Publishing Company. "Devotionals don't sell well anyway." Doubt clouded my mind. But to my surprise, we had to order a second printing before the year was half over. Encouraging comments came in—letters from old friends as well as new ones.

The next year while looking for files for my husband, I ran across several pioneer women stories which had never been published; so I began working on *Pioneer Pentecostal Women, Volume III*, which was published in 2003.

Then I began reading about hope. What an encouragement that was! For the past two years, I have studied and written on this subject. My prayer is that it will bless you and give you hope for today and faith for tomorrow.

Charles Sawyer said, "Of all the forces that make for a better world none is so indispensable, none so powerful, as hope. Without hope, men are half alive. With hope they think and dream and work." Hope sustains us. Hope is the building block of faith. Hope gives us reason to push on when the devil and his cohorts try to trap us.

Especially in today's world, people are at risk of losing hope. In the last two years, my husband had forty-five radiation treatments for prostate cancer. Then he had a tumor removed from his brain. Thank God, it was benign. I had two major stomach surgeries. In the last two months, J. O.'s cancer has returned and our dear daughter-in-law, Joanne, has developed colon cancer. But we keep hoping and trusting in the mighty God in Christ, who is worthy of our trust and hope.

May this book keep you hoping and trusting and looking to Jesus, the author and finisher of our faith.

Acknowledgments

This is my nineteenth book and my first book on a biblical subject, hope—an important subject in today's stress-filled world. As I said in the preface, since writing on this subject, we have faced major stress with my husband's cancer, a brain tumor, my severe stomach surgeries, then more recently our daughter-in-law's battle with colon cancer.

Thank God for His presence and for His Word that is filled with hope which sustains us. Thanks also to many other writers who have written great books on this subject.

Before I retired from the Pentecostal Publishing House in 1992, my dear daughter, Margie, took time to teach me the basics of word processing on a computer. Am I ever grateful! Also for my dear eldest son, Jim, who patiently helps me when I lose copy or when I need special computer help in other ways. A special thanks to my son, Jeffrey, who built this lovely sunroom which my husband and I share. Thanks to all six children: Jim, Margie, Jack, Jeff, Rosemary, and Joe who have given us a computer, printer, scanner, and a desk, as well as lots of encouragement!

Thanks to my dear mother, Maria Weedman Hardwick, and my grandmother, Annie Fuqua Weedman, who accepted the Pentecostal message when it was first preached in 1916 in my hometown, Finley, Tennessee. They brought me up in the fear of God and gave me hope beyond that small town in Tennessee.

A special thanks to Barbara Washburn, Brian Stewart,

Janice Jentzsch, Peggy Jenkins, and Mrs. Ronald Schneider for sharing their touching stories about God's help and hope in their lives.

A very special thanks to my dear husband, J. O., who has always encouraged my writing and helped open doors for me in his ministry with the UPCI Sunday School Division and the Pentecostal Publishing House.

CHAPTER 1

We've Gotta Have Hope

In Jeremiah 12:1, the prophet asked, "Wherefore doth the way of the wicked prosper?" When the righteous suffer, why is God silent? Where is His justice? Is there any hope in this life? The writer of Proverbs declared that "Hope deferred maketh the heart sick" (Proverbs 13:12). Indeed, loss of hope is a killer. We've gotta have hope!

At age fourteen, I saw a shocking scene of no hope. My mother and I went to the Tennessee Pentecostal camp meeting with our pastor and his family. Late at night, we returned to find our house well lit. My father's two brothers and their families were returning from Chicago. In Kentucky a truck without lights and loaded with pottery crashed into them, killing my Uncle Mack, his wife and baby. Everyone in the car died except a girl and Uncle Johnny, the driver. Badly burned, he was hospitalized for months.

After the funeral, my aunt Anna sat to write the tragic news to her younger sister who lived in California. Suddenly she pounded the table, then screamed, "I can't! I can't!" So I had to write the bad news. Aunt Anna had no hope!

In contrast, recently my friend, Pearl Reed, a great prayer warrior, suffered a severe shock. A train hit and killed her grandson. Sister Reed's face looked lined with grief. She returned my hug and softly said, "God is good!" Hope in God's mercy and goodness held her steady.

Hope is to life what seeds are to the earth. We cannot be fruitful without hope. Life is sterile without hope. Dreams die and destinies are derailed without hope. Even faith is the substance of things *hoped* for. In that great chapter, Paul wrote in I Corinthians 13:13, faith and love are linked by one weak word, *hope*.

George Frederic Watts painted the famous picture called *Hope* of a blindfolded woman sitting on the world with only one star in the sky, stricken and dejected. In her hand is a harp with all the strings broken except one. She is striking that one string and listening carefully to its sound. The artist named the painting simply *Hope*.[1] When the world, the flesh, and the devil seem to take everything, we must listen carefully for the sound of one note of hope.

Years ago I read the story of an abandoned baby boy in an American hospital. An English war bride named May, a nurse in the hospital, took the baby. Others did not think the infant would even live. The little boy was seven or eight years old before May could toilet train him. He could not talk. Finally he learned to walk by holding to a fence.

One day May noticed him plucking in a rhythmic way on one piece of string. "He might respond to music," she thought. She bought an old upright piano and began to play some of the popular tunes she had played in army camps for the soldiers in England. After she went to bed, she woke, astounded to hear the music that she had played coming from the piano. Then she discovered that the boy could play anything once he heard it. Later he learned to sing. Finally he learned to talk. Music brought May's boy hope.

I have never forgotten that touching story of May's boy. At one of the Christian booksellers' conventions which I attended, May's boy played the piano. Unfortunately I was not able to hear him, but friends said he was fabulous. One string of hope brought triumph out of tragedy.

My mother studied classical piano and had a great collection of music until Grandmother Weedman's house burned. One sheet of popular music, "Whispering Hope," survived. I don't know what finally happened to that music, but I remember as a teenager picking out the melody with one finger. I still recall some of the words:

> Soft as the voice of an angel, breathing a lesson unheard,
> Hope with a gentle persuasion whispers her comforting word. . . .
> Whispering hope, O how welcome thy voice,
> Making my heart in its sorrow rejoice.

I wonder if my mother bought that music after my baby sister died suddenly at only nine months old.

No one gets through this life without suffering loss of hope or having hope deferred. Loss of hope is the common "cold" of the soul, except this virus can kill.

If you cannot change your circumstances, change the way you respond. Learn to relish small, daily, simple things like sitting on a porch. Our front porch helped us find hope the summer of 2002 when I had serious stomach surgery. Then my husband, who had survived forty-five radiation treatments for prostate cancer, fell out of the bed. X rays revealed no broken bones, but my daughter, Rosemary, who is a nurse, insisted on a CAT scan. "Dad is not one to stumble around," she said.

The CAT scan revealed a tumor on the front of his brain. Dr. Standard operated and removed the tumor. Thank God, it was neither entwined nor malignant. However, temporarily J. O. lost a lot of memory. I tried not to reveal my concern when the therapist questioned him with simple questions. He did not even know his own birthday! We sat on the front porch in the sunshine for hours, looked up to blue skies and found hope for better days. As the doctors had assured us, J. O.'s memory returned. I tease him now and tell him that he remembers things that I am not sure even happened. Thank God for blue skies and a front porch! We had to have hope.

Hope builds churches. Christians first met in homes, then catacombs, then finally the Vatican in Rome. American pioneers built log cabin homes, then churches.

Hope sows seeds of desire for schools. In 1639 not too long after the first settlement in America in 1620, the Puritans started Harvard as a school to train ministers. Later in 1718, Yale was founded, then Princeton.

In the 1940s, the Jews in Hitler's labor camps on

their way to Auschwitz taught their children. "Perhaps some of them will escape." Teachers planted seeds of hope that better days would come. Elie Wiesel, one young man who did escape, later wrote great books verifying the horrors of the Holocaust.

Hope builds hospitals. At first simple clinics, such as Albert Schweitzer built in Africa, later hospitals across the world. Researchers looked for cures for diseases. After two hundred trials, Jonas Salk finally found a vaccine that conquered polio. Others keep looking for a cancer cure. We all hope and pray that they will find it soon! Cancer crushes the hopes of so many.

Hope of finding a better route to the East sent Christopher Columbus sailing into the unknown. Hope caused space engineers to reach for the stars, and then they landed on the moon. Explorers began exploring with a dream. They had to have hope!

Young girls with unwanted pregnancies lose hope, seek abortions, then spend a lifetime crying about the lost baby. Often poor medical help prevents some of these girls from having other children, causing more pain. A friend of mine, Kim Stone, wrote a book, *I Have a Secret*, about a similar experience in her own life. Thankfully she found forgiveness and she and her husband adopted two beautiful children. She wrote the book to bring a seed of hope to other young women.

Divorce destroys dreams and hope. Families split, suffering lost hopes, destruction of dreams, not to mention helpless children torn between the love of each parent. Listen to the groans and moans of drug addicts, the homeless as well as the frustrated excuses of the driven and overworked and underpaid. We've gotta have hope!

Unfortunately these moans and groans create almost a symphony of sorrow. They can even be heard in church when child abuse by priests and pastors make national news. On December 3, 2002, *The Tennessean* carried more bad news of this nature concerning a priest in Boston who taught young girls learning to be nuns how to be more spiritual by loving him intimately as they would Jesus as the bride of Christ. The abuse was bad, but cover-up by the authorities in charge allowed the priest to be transferred to another parish and continue the abuse. Teenage pregnancies and marital breakups happen in many churches.

Does this information seem hopeless? Yes. That is why I have been researching and studying the subject of hope. Because so many of today's people need hope. Stay with me and let's find out why some people lose hope and how we can sow seeds of hope in today's society. We've gotta have hope!

In the book, *The Heart of America*, by Mike Trout, he tells a story of a woman who lost hope and almost divorced her husband. "I wrote a letter to *Focus on the Family*, and a counselor called me and talked to me for over an hour on the phone. That was a powerful influence on my life. My family is still intact today and oh, what I would have missed if I had destroyed my family." She found a seed of hope because someone took time to listen.

I heard the testimony of the last person who was rescued from the World Trade Center. Janelle McMillan lay trapped twenty-seven hours in a one-in-a-million air pocket in the WTC. *Time* magazine carried her story, "The Last Survivor." Janelle testified that she was a party girl from Trinidad. Although she had attended Brooklyn Tabernacle, pastored by Jim Cymbala, she said, "I did not want to live

for God—too many rules. Church was for old people."
Raised as a Catholic, she said she did not know how to pray.
"I knew 'The Lord Is My Shepherd' and that's about all."
From the sixty-fourth floor, she rushed down to the thir-
teenth, stopped to take off her shoes, then heard the sound
of the building collapsing around her. She felt herself falling
as literally tons of blazing twisted metal, shattered glass and
concrete came tumbling around her. She was trapped! "I
could only move my left arm. I did not know how to pray. I
begged God for a second chance, and He heard my cry."

Finally after twenty-seven hours, she heard someone
digging nearby. She tapped with a broken shard and heard
a voice. She pushed one finger through the rubble and made
contact with a valiant New York firefighter who grabbed her
finger and cried, "I've got you!" Trapped for twenty-seven
hours, she never gave up hope. Later she went to the
Brooklyn Tabernacle and gave her life to God. Now she tes-
tifies of the hope found in the mighty God in Christ.

The Ronald Schneider family desperately needed
hope in March 2000. Ron Jr. woke up on the 27th feeling
bad. He had a doctor's appointment for a check-up, but
traffic was so terrible that they missed his appointment.
His mother tells the story:

"We came back home and Ron lay down for a while.
We had a dinner appointment which I offered to cancel,
but he wanted to go. After dinner we prayed, then Ron
went downstairs to play some video games. Later he grew
worse with fever, chills, and breathing problems, so we
went to the emergency room at St. John's Mercy hospital
in St. Louis. 'Pneumonia,' they said as they hooked him to
oxygen. The next morning before leaving for work, I

called. He seemed okay. But by the time my husband and I got off work, our pastor, Brother Rudy Theissen, called and said, 'They're moving Ron to Intensive Care Unit.'

"When we got there, the ICU doctor told us they needed to put Ron on a ventilator. 'His heart rate is racing and his blood pressure is rising.' They sedated him and that was the last time we were able to talk to him for about three or four weeks. He grew worse each day.

"The doctor said, 'Seventy percent of patients as sick as Ron don't make it.'

"'We have a wonderful church full of people who are praying for our boy. He's going to walk out of here. When you folks give up, our God will take over and Ron will walk out of here!' declared Ron's dad.

"During this time, Ron's lungs were not distributing enough oxygen to sustain his vital organs. Everything started shutting down. His heart rate raced. His blood pressure dropped. His bowels shut down. His stomach swelled and pushed against his diaphragm, causing more breathing difficulty. When we even touched him, his vital signs went crazy. So they put him in a drug-induced coma so that machines could do all the work for him.

"He was in isolation, and we had to wear masks and gloves and were told not to touch him. I managed to touch him gently, sing a familiar gospel song and pray. We stayed in the ICU waiting room all the time. We'd sleep an hour, then go stand at the door, watch him and check on all the monitors. Tests revealed that Ron had Influenza Type A, so they started a new medication. He had so many wires and machines hooked to him that they had to label and date them to keep track of them. They tried steroids but he swelled even more.

"'We're running out of options,' the ICU doctors said. 'We have a new experimental gas we'd like to try.'

"'Let us pray about it,' we said, then called the church for prayer for wisdom. We signed papers acknowledging that this was experimental and might not work. It worked! His oxygen level stabilized, and they were able to bring him out of the drug coma.

"Usually I woke early to read my Bible and pray as I sat in a window facing a garden below. Beautiful blooming flowers and trees helped me to have hope. Each day I read a psalm searching for and underlining positive scriptures. Ron's doctor noticed my Bible reading. 'Does it help?' he asked.

"'Tremendously,' I assured him.

"'It will be a long, slow recovery,' he warned. They moved him out of ICU, but a secondary pneumonia developed so back he went to ICU.

"After six weeks of ups and downs, Ron was finally ready to recuperate. Two weeks later he was ready for rehab. Finally after eleven weeks as his dad had said, Ron did go home healed! Through all our trials, our family has come to know that the blessed hope in Jesus is the best thing that has ever happened to us."

Stephen Staten, M.D. gave the Schneiders a beautiful letter acknowledging how sick Ron had been. "I am sure, without a doubt, having witnessed this firsthand myself that Ronald and his family's faith in God and strong commitment to prayer are probably the ultimate reason that he survived his serious medical illness."

The Schneiders' testimony bears witness to the beautiful voice of faith and hope in Christ Jesus. In times like these, we've gotta have hope!

Sow Seeds of Hope

Listen carefully for that voice of hope. In the middle of chaos and crumbling dreams, His voice can still be heard, saying, "For the Son of man is come to seek and to save that which was lost" (Luke 19:10), seeds of hope spoken by the Savior.

Our churches can still reach out to hospitals and doctors and to a lost world and plant seeds of hope with the good news of the gospel. Many churches are growing, building new buildings, planting daughter churches. Facilities are expanding. Church budgets are mounting. Big billboards announce special meetings. Others, however, seem to be splitting although they are too small to split. What is the problem? What can we do about those who are lost in church? Second Chronicles 7:14 promises, "If my people, which are called by my name, shall humble themselves, and pray, and seek my face, and turn from their wicked ways; then will I hear from heaven, and will forgive their sin, and will heal their land." Repentance and commitment sow seeds of new hope. These seeds must be watered with tears of repentance.

During trouble we need hope and deliverance from fear. Isaiah 44:2 says, "Thus saith the LORD that made thee, and formed thee from the womb, which will help thee; Fear not."

Little foxes of negligence can steal our spiritual joy and victory. Our world is filled with poisons that cause depression, doubt and despair. Just a little infection can drain our body of health. A chronic cough may mask deadly cancer. A mole or wart changing shape and color may be a forerunner of melanoma. Little poisonous rattlesnakes or brown recluse spiders can be fatal. Better to light a candle of hope than to curse the darkness. We've gotta have hope!

Believe the gospel. Romans 15:4, "For whatsoever things were written aforetime were written for our learning, that we through patience and comfort of the scriptures might have *hope*" (italics added). Romans 10:9, "If thou shalt confess with thy mouth the Lord Jesus, and shalt believe in thine heart that God hath raised him from the dead, thou shalt be saved." John 8:24, "I said therefore unto you, that ye shall die in your sins: for if ye believe not that I am he, ye shall die in your sins." Acts 2:38, "Then Peter said unto them, Repent, and be baptized every one of you in the name of Jesus Christ for the remission of sins, and ye shall receive the gift of the Holy Ghost." Now that's eternal hope!

Once I greeted an elderly man saying, "It's a beautiful day!" He replied, "Any day I can crawl out of bed is a great day." Then he told me about his wife who was bedfast for two years before she died. That man knew he had to have hope.

Norman Cousins said, "A man can live ten minutes without air, two days without water, forty days without food but not a single second without hope." Dr. Bernie Siegler, oncology surgeon said, "The only false hope is no hope." We've gotta have hope!

Hebrews 6:18-19, "That . . . we might have a strong consolation, who have fled for refuge to lay hold upon the hope set before us: which hope we have as an anchor of the soul, both sure and stedfast." Remember that grand old hymn, "My Anchor Holds."

As I am working on this book, there is famine in Africa, floods in China and India and Germany. We worry about the Middle East. Will there be another oil crisis? The year 2003 began our war in Iraq. Mosquitoes spread West Nile epidemic in Louisiana. Anthrax packages in the mail killed people. A strange new disease in China kills dozens. The certainty and finality of death casts a pall of hopelessness over many. Cancer clinics are crowded. People sue tobacco companies for their own addictions. One obese patient is suing McDonalds for selling fattening foods. Others place their hope on a lottery where there is less than one chance in ten thousand.

A Harvard Medical School professor, Dr. Armand Mayo Nicholi II, said in an article in *Christianity Today*, "The word 'hope' is used and heard little in our culture. Perhaps hope conflicts with our concept of a scientific world. Many books exist on faith and on love, but few on hope."

Psychiatrist Karl Menninger writes, "In scientific circles there is a determined effort to exclude hope from conceptual thinking . . . because of a fear of corrupting objective judgment by wishful thinking. But all science is built on hope, so much so that science is for many moderns a substitute . . . Man can't help hoping even if he is a scientist. He can only hope more accurately."[2]

The study of hope is an area "very much undeveloped in psychology."

Yet we know we've gotta have hope. Hope is absolutely essential. Hope of a better life for her son led the Cuban mother to tie her small son to an inner tube. She left him floating off the coast of Florida although she herself drowned.

In prison on Christmas Day, Jimmy Bakker cleaned toilets, hope almost gone, feeling guilty and hopeless. "You have visitors," he was told. Billy Graham and his wife, Ruth, took time from a family holiday to bring hope to a fallen minister.

Theologian Emil Brunner said, "What oxygen is for the lungs, such is hope for the meaning of human life. Take oxygen away and death occurs through suffocation; take hope away and humanity is constricted through lack of breath; despair supervenes, spelling the paralysis of intellectual and spiritual powers by a feeling of sense-lessness and purposelessness of existence. As the fate of the human organism is dependent on the supply of oxy-gen, so the fate of humanity is dependent on its supply of hope."[3]

A church carries this inscription:

> In the year 1653, when all things sacred were throughout the Nation either demolished or profaned, Sir Robert Shirley Barronet founded this church; Whose singular praise it is to have done the best things in the worst times and to have hoped them in the most calamitous.[4]

To keep hoping during the bad times is today's chal-lenge to Christians as it was in 1653! Wars and rumors of wars seem just as prevalent today as ever. The U.S. troops still search for Osama bin Laden in Afghanistan. Our troops have captured Saddam Hussein, but they are still fighting terrorists in Iraq. President Bush declared vic-tory, but snipers are still killing our occupation troops. Is there any hope for peace in the Middle East? Who has the answer?

We often question, Where is my hope? as Job did in chapter 17:15. We feel lost in the dark and wonder what have we ever done to deserve the trials we go through. "Why?" is the wrong question. The right question is "How can I learn from this horrible happening what God is trying to teach me?"

Solomon said in Ecclesiastes 9:12, "So are the sons of men snared in an evil time, when it falleth suddenly upon them." Paul said, "Now we see through a glass, darkly." But as the old gospel song sung during the Great Depression days says, "We will understand it better by and by."

Suffering is part of the human condition. Suffering took Jesus all alone, rejected and despised to the ignominious cruel cross, yet today that cross has become a plus symbol of hope and is reared high atop churches all around the world. Once a symbol of shame, today the cross is a symbol of hope!

Paul told us in I Corinthians 15:19 that "If in this life only we have hope in Christ, we are of all men most miserable." We've gotta have hope! Horrible things can and do happen when we lose hope.

CHAPTER 2

Horrible Things Happen without Hope

Horrible things often happen when we lose hope. Doubt, depression, and despair can lead to devastation and complete destruction—even suicide.

According to the Center for Disease Control, suicide is one of the major causes of death in America. The rate keeps growing. Suicide is the second leading cause of death among college students and the third leading cause of death among children. Fatherless homes account for over sixty percent of youth suicides, ninety percent of homeless/runaway children, and over eighty percent of youths in prison. The youth suicide rate has tripled in the past thirty-five years.

Recently my son-in-law, Joel, had a call from his mother in Mississippi concerning one of her friends at church. "Helen Sims (not her real name) just shot and killed herself. We don't know all the details, but she called 911, told them to pick up her body—that she would be dead when they arrived." Helen's husband had died two years before. Joel spoke at his funeral. Left alone, Helen lived with her daughter and attended a Pentecostal church. We don't know what caused her to became so depressed. Apparently she lost all hope and just decided to end it all. Helen desperately needed someone to sow seeds of hope in her life.

In his November 20, 2002, column of *The Tennessean*, Frank Ritter's doctor insisted that he go to the apartment of a friend to retrieve a noose stored in a closet. "I don't want that noose hanging in that apartment. He's suffering severe depression and wonders whether life's worth living."

Doctors, counselors, pastors, and close friends listen and hold hands when patients, church members, and friends as they pour out their stories of doubt, despair, and despondency. Loss of hope can definitely cause horrible things to happen.

Depression is a major problem in the U.S. The pharmaceutical companies may be the only ones who are reaping rewards from all our troubles with depression, as we spend thousands of dollars on pill after pill.

Hopelessness can attack the prosperous as well as the poverty-stricken. David Shibley in his book, *Ultimate Success*, tells about his friend, Jim. Jim had it all. "Handsome, likeable, all-star back on our football team, a diligent student who dated the prettiest cheerleader. He drove a Corvette Stingray when he wasn't on his Harley." He sat next to David in accounting class, and David started to share his faith with Jim. "Come on over to my house tonight. I want to hear more." So David drove his mother's old Ford Falcon over and spent an hour sharing the gospel with Jim. Finally Jim took a deep breath and responded, "David, I'm glad it works for you. But, man, look what I've got. Look at who I am. I'm on a social merry-go-round, and I don't have time to get off this ride and think about anything else. Thanks, anyway, David, but I really don't want to hear any more about this Jesus stuff."

A few months later a friend asked David, "Have you heard about Jim?"

"Only that he's getting ready to go to college on a football scholarship," David answered.

"Well, they found him yesterday in a field. He put a rifle in his mouth and blew his brains out."[1]

Some people let fear paralyze them. As a young mother living on Michigan Avenue in St. Louis, I remember washing dishes in the kitchen, when I heard the front door open. I rushed through the dining room. In the middle of the living room stood a stranger with a basket on his arm. "What in the world do you want?" I yelled.

He looked startled, then said, "I must be in the wrong house!"

"You certainly are!" I said firmly and followed him as he backed out the front door. I slammed the door quickly and locked it. From that day to this, I always keep the front door locked. Later I shook with fear, but the Lord gave me courage to bluff that man right out of my house.

Safety and security cannot be taken for granted. The

eighty-six-year-old mother of a friend of mine fell victim to a roofing scam. The man cheated her out of several thousand dollars. A few days later when the elderly woman was in the backyard working, the man returned, went into her house and stole five hundred dollars more. "I really don't know how much he stole. It may have been over two thousand dollars," Dorothy told me.

My father fell victim to a similar scam when he was in his eighties. The thief stole Dad's checkbook. When he tried to cash a check, an alert grocery man noticed the name and called my brother. Crimes, violence, storms, and tornadoes seem to fill our days. We find ourselves losing hope and living in fear.

Fear made ten men feel like grasshoppers as these spies confessed when Moses sent them to spy out Canaan. "Slavery in Egypt is better than this," they thought foolishly. They paid for their lack of faith by serving forty more years in the desert! Caleb and Joshua bravely sowed seeds of hope and courage; Caleb and Joshua reaped homes in the Promised Land!

My husband's cousin, Lunelle Shelby, married a farmer named Raymond whose first wife had committed suicide. The woman was convinced that she had cancer although her doctor had said, "No." She left two children, a girl named Janet and a boy named Gerald.

After his wife's death, the farmer married Lunelle, who had worked her way through college and got a master's degree in teaching. She was justly proud of her bright teenaged stepchildren. The boy graduated as valedictorian of Scotts Hill High School and was accepted as a pre-med student at Memphis State University. The university was a big step up from the Decatur County High

School. Gerald's grades dropped due to higher competition. Very discouraged he switched majors to agriculture and enrolled in a smaller college.

A fine Pentecostal boy, Gerald played his guitar in church and had a Pentecostal girlfriend. We don't know exactly what happened. Was it a lover's quarrel or a feeling of rejection from the med school? Whatever the reason, he must have lost hope. He drove a back road to his father's farm, pulled into the carport and went to the closet where stood the rifle that his mother had used. Also in that closet, his father kept the overalls that he wore when feeding the animals. The next morning when his father opened the closet door to get his work clothes, Gerald's body tumbled out. He had killed himself with the same rifle his mother had used.

At that funeral, tears filled the eyes of even the small-town funeral director. That was the first close acquaintance I ever had with a suicide. I wondered what in the world had caused Gerald to feel so hopeless. He had everything to live for: a fine sister, a loving father with a big farm, and a stepmother who was very proud of him, not to mention a respected name in that small community with a host of friends. What happened? Why did he lose hope?

Various things can cause people to lose hope. Recently a man came into the bookstore where I work. As we talked, he told me of his experience with depression. He had pastored a Presbyterian church and had helped many people while pastoring. He had experienced the power of the Holy Ghost and knew what it could do for people. He didn't say why he left the ministry.

Later he became a captain on the metro police force

and served there for twenty-eight years. He drifted away from God. Problems piled up. In 2000 he was so depressed that the authorities sent him to a psychologist for a battery of tests. As a result, he was forced to take early retirement.

He went home and went to bed. He slept ten hours a day, didn't want to leave his room, didn't want to take a bath, grew a beard, didn't want to eat, worried about finance, thought he was dying, and considered suicide.

One day he sat up in bed and thought, "I don't want to die. I want to live! I am God's child. He still loves me." He realized that Satan was trying to destroy him. "I remembered Bible verses I had learned as a child. I knew God was with me. Systematically I began to do things. Left my room, went downstairs to my family. My wife began to take me for short drives. Before, I felt like the trees were closing in on me, now I enjoyed nature. I got better and went back to church. We attended Hallelujah Acres in Shelby, North Carolina, and learned about health and nutrition. Now I am active in a prayer group, enjoying life again. But I know that horrible depression can definitely kill a man!"

Discouraging words can kill the seeds of hope. In his book, *Head First*, Norman Cousins tells of a Los Angeles woman who went to her doctor when she developed a chest cough. Her physician put her through all sorts of tests, including X rays. On the basis of the tests, the doctor said, "You have about sixty days to live." The immediate effect was catastrophic. She had been working, but she went into deep depression, stopped eating, lost eighteen pounds in a little more than a week.

Then she consulted another physician, who told her

that medical journals regularly carry reports of cancer patients who recovered altogether or inexplicably lived much longer than their doctors had predicted. He concentrated on providing the best treatment and encouraging the woman. At the time Cousins wrote his book, the lady was still living.[2]

When my husband, J. O., was diagnosed with prostate cancer, he had to go to the hospital five days a week for radiation. How I dreaded our first trip to that cancer clinic. To my surprise, the nurses and the doctors had a very cheerful, upbeat attitude. No gloom and doom in St. Thomas Cancer Clinic. In fact the nurses were almost downright flirtatious! Always laughing and teasing, despite the patients' bald heads, thin bodies, and other signs of sickness. Their goal was to build hope and beat that cancer!

When my father developed Alzheimer's, we had to find nursing care for him. Within a short while, Dad quit eating. The nurses told my son that he cried for two weeks. While working in St. Louis, I tried to fly down to visit him at least every other month. I noticed that he was losing weight. When we checked it, he had lost thirty-five pounds! It's hard to eat when you have no purpose, no reason to try. A loss of hope leads to despair that delivers deep depression which can lead to death. Sometimes the severity of the depression is not noticeable to loved ones. Dad only lived about eighteen months in the nursing home.

Recently I met a woman whose son had committed suicide. Rejected by his girlfriend because he didn't have a career, he became deeply depressed. His stepfather called him a loser, and he did not have a good relationship with his father and stepmother. His mother tried to slip money to him to avoid aggravating her husband. The young man could only find work in construction, which he felt was a dead-end street. Apparently he could not set academic or career goals. He visited with his mother and told her that he didn't know what to do. He drove off, parked his car with the windows rolled up, went to sleep and died of carbon monoxide poison. That boy desperately needed a seed of hope.

In his book, *Tell Your Heart to Beat Again*, Dutch Sheets says that almost twenty million adults have a depressive disorder, and the leading cause of disability is major depressive disorder. Eighty percent of adult children of pastors seek professional help for depression. Fifty percent of pastors would leave the ministry if they could find other ways to make a living. Over a thousand pastors leave the ministry each month.[3] They lose hope.

Perhaps this is true only in denominational church. However, it sounds a warning to all of us. We must seek the joy of the Holy Ghost daily and resist all feelings of hopelessness. The joy of the Lord is our strength.

In the February 2002 *Reader's Digest*, Sue Ellen Browder wrote that people with serious depression are three times more likely to have heart problems. In fact depression is equal to smoking a pack of cigarettes a day. We must resist depression and cling to Him.

Abraham and Sarah experienced "deferred hope." The promised son did not arrive, so Sarah tried to second-guess God. We are all still suffering from the trouble she caused when Ishmael was born. His descendants are the Arabs, who hate the Jews as well as Americans who support Jews. So they train terrorists to do horrible things like blowing up the World Trade Center.

One can understand why Abraham and Sarah got discouraged. They were already old, but God made them wait ten years longer. Talk about hope deferred! They laughed cynically, but God had the last laugh. Abraham and Sarah certainly learned that where there's life, there's a seed of hope!

Moses became fearful and depressed after he killed the Egyptian. He fled from the king's palace to the back side of the desert. Forty years later when God spoke to him from a burning bush, Moses stuttered and stammered and made all kinds of excuses. Who am I? Actually he was a backside-of-the-desert cynic. After all, he had been herding sheep for forty years. His princely self-confidence was long since gone. Finally Moses learned that he was God's man.

Read his epitaph in Deuteronomy 34:10. "And there arose not a prophet since in Israel like unto Moses, whom the Lord knew face to face." From hopelessness to triumph!

In a recent sermon, Pastor Ron Becton told that in grammar school, the two biggest boys were chosen to lead the ball teams. The smallest, most awkward boy was chosen last.

David was the kid chosen last. At first even Samuel believed in Saul to the point that God had to tell him outright that He had rejected the tall, handsome king. Concerning the search for a new king, "The Lord said unto Samuel, Look not on his countenance, or on the height of his stature; because I have refused him: for the Lord seeth not as man seeth; for man looketh on the outward appearance, but the Lord looketh on the heart" (I Samuel 16:7).

David had much against him. A curse on him before

he was born? He was a third-generation Moabite. A generational curse? Did David have questions about his birth? "I was shapen in iniquity; and in sin did my mother conceive me" (Psalm 51:5). Was this the reason he was not even brought into Samuel as a son? David's brothers belittled him.

In a sermon about David and the giant, a minister said, "We all need giants in our lives. They bring out the best in us just as Goliath did for David. Giants will bring opportunities in your life. As long as life is mundane and routine, we are not challenged to do our best. Giants make you stand out from the crowd. Crowds sometimes lead to destruction and lost victory. The crowd of Israelites stayed in the wilderness for forty years doing the same old routine. Goliath and the Philistines had a fixed fight, but David found a cause that challenged him. Until we meet a giant in our lives, life will always be run of the mill. Why follow the sniveling scared crowds? Pick up that sling and let God use you as He did David."

After David killed Goliath, he became a favorite at the palace, playing skillfully on his harp while moody Saul suffered from depression. Saul heard the people singing about his killing thousands but David ten thousands. Jealousy burned Saul and he sought to kill David, the shepherd, the giant-killer, and the harpist. (Song of Solomon 8:6, "Jealousy is cruel as the grave.")

First Samuel 27:10 found David hiding from the jealous King Saul. He sought refuge with Israel's enemies, the Philistines. He and his six hundred men had located at Gath with King Achish. They made war on Achish's enemies. After one raid, Achish asked David, "Whither have ye made a road to day?" What have you done today,

David? A hard question for David. He may have asked himself, "Who am I? A Philistine or an Israelite? What am I doing in Gath? Where am I going? I'm tired of running."

Doubtless David was depressed and devastated. He feared destruction by King Saul. It had been a long trail from the back pasture where he had watched his father's sheep. Many months and even years had passed since Samuel had anointed David as king. "Where are you, God?" He wrote, "Why art thou cast down, O my soul? and why art thou disquieted in me? hope thou in God" (Psalm 42:5). Some of his Psalms, 42, 43, and 142, were perhaps written in the cave where he fled from the jealous King Saul. These writings reflect his doubts and questions.

Later after Saul was gone and David occupied the throne and fought the Philistines, he took a holiday and fell into sin with Bathsheba. But David always called on the Lord even in his sin, "Against thee, thee only, have I sinned. . . . Create in me a clean heart, O God; and renew a right spirit within me" (Psalm 51:4, 10). No final despair, no finger pointing, no blame! David accepted responsibility for his actions, turned to God, and found forgiveness, peace, and seeds of hope.

In Luke 4:18, Jesus said, "The Spirit of the Lord is upon me, because he hath anointed me to preach the gospel to the poor; he hath sent me to heal the *broken-hearted*" (italics added). Jesus came to bring hope to hearts that were broken by horrible happenings.

Several things cause men and women to lose hope such as discouragement, lack of purpose, confusion (I don't know what to do with my life), disillusionment, and bitterness. This leads to cynicism and a complete loss of faith and hope—a truly broken heart.

On the back of the book, *Tell Your Heart to Beat Again*, by Dutch Sheets, he tells the story of an open-heart surgery that his brother was allowed to witness. The patient's heart had been stopped from beating. When it was time to restart the patient's heart, the medical staff was unable to get it beating again. Although the patient was obviously unconscious, the surgeon leaned over and whispered into the patient's ear. "We need your help. We cannot get your heart going. Tell your heart to start beating." Incredibly, the patient's heart immediately began to beat again.[4]

I once knew a nice family of five people: mother, father, grandmother, brother, and a sister. The father was a talented man, successful in his career. The mother seemed to be a good mother and housewife. I lost track of them for a while, then heard that the couple had divorced. The father moved into his own apartment; the boy found his own place; the grandmother living in a nursing home. Only the mother and daughter still lived together. Divorce wreaked havoc on that home. A happy family of five wound up in three apartments and a nursing home.

A promise not kept, betrayal, rejection, or false accusation can cause loss of hope. A friend of mine had a daughter who accused her minister father of abuse. Child welfare officials removed her from her Christian home. This did not solve her problems at all. Later she was tragically killed in an automobile accident. No family escapes problems; only the grace of God keeps us hoping.

A failed marriage often causes a horrible loss of hope. One writer said that the divorce rate has risen 279 percent in the last twenty-seven years. Divorce seems to inevitably lead to deep depression. The loss of a stable home causes many fears, depression, and grief in the children of divorce.

Lonely singles struggle with rejection. Women striving to achieve in the business world put off marriage and children. Then facing the ticking of the biological clock, they begin to long for a home and a family. *The Tennessean* recently carried the story of a very successful career woman in her middle fifties who finally adopted four children. "These children have brought me more happiness than anything else," she declared.

Accidents, disease, and physical ailments can cause deep depression. Tim Hansel in his book, *You Gotta Keep Dancin'*, tells of his mountain climbing accident which resulted in major damage to his body. "I can't remember when I have woke up feeling good. Perhaps this is the ultimate realization—when we recognize that all the questions have the same answer. I don't understand what or why or where you are taking me, Lord. But grant me the strength to either surrender or defy it all. Should it serve your strong purpose, continue to break me."[5]

The death of a loved one often causes loss of hope. After my mother died in 1977, Dad's doctor told us that a widower or a widow usually died within two years of the death of his mate. Dad faced his lot after he had to undergo minor surgery about a year after Mom's death. As he recovered, he also regained his desire to live and lived ten more years to age eighty-seven.

A family member who is still unsaved may seem hopeless. I can still hear the screams of Sister Jones. (Names have been changed.) Her son, Tom, was a classmate of mine. We had just graduated from grammar school and were in our annual summer revival. Brother E. E. McNatt had preached the gospel and was giving the altar call. He went back and spoke to Tom, but the boy turned to leave the building. As he stepped on the porch of the little white frame church, another friend greeted him and slapped him on the back. Tom dropped dead! That summer I made my calling and election sure, was baptized in Jesus' name and filled with the Holy Ghost. I knew my hope was built on nothing less than Jesus and His righteousness!

It's hard to deal with pain, frustration, and fear. The disillusionment in our own abilities is perhaps one of the most important things that can happen to us. What a test of character adversity is! It can either destroy or build up, depending upon our chosen response. Pain can make us either better or bitter.

Young children used to worry about the atom bomb. Now they visualize terrorists, snipers, and planes flying into buildings.

Third-world countries suffer from famine. Ten thousand a week die of starvation. AIDS is a major problem in Africa as well as India and China. Now China and even Canada are in the grip of fear of SARS. Who knows how far that will spread.

Lloyd Ogilvie in his great book, *A Future and a Hope*, says, "What we think about controls our outlook on life—our attitudes, how we look at the problems and potentials of life, our relationships, and what we dare to expect that the Lord can do to help us. In between the impact of what's happening to and around us, there is a split-second mental response that triggers how we perceive things, how we feel, and how we react.

"Our thinking determines how well we will survive in a battle we must fight all of our lives. There can never be a truce. This battle is with discouragement, the antagonist of hope. It's one of the most deadly weapons of the force of evil."[6]

In Matthew 16:21-23, Jesus tried to explain to His disciples how that He must suffer, but Peter with human emotion and feeling tried to rebuke Jesus saying, "Be it far from thee, Lord." Jesus immediately turned and said to Peter, "Get thee behind me, Satan." Jesus knew full well the part He was to play in redemption, and He had no time for discouragement.

The January 1995 issue of *Guideposts* included this quote from Vance Havner, "It takes broken soil to produce a crop, broken clouds to give rain, broken grain to give bread, broken bread to give strength. It is the broken alabaster box that gives forth perfume—it is Peter, (broken) weeping bitterly, who returns to greater power than ever."

Matthew recorded the story of Peter and Judas. In chapter 26:31-35, after the Last Supper when Judas left Jesus and the other apostles, they went out to the Mount of Olives. There Jesus said that "all ye shall be offended because of me this night." Peter stoutly contradicted the Lord, saying, "Though I should die with thee, yet will I not deny thee." All the disciples said the same thing. But Luke 22:32 records that Jesus said, "I have prayed for thee, that thy faith fail not." Oh, blessed hope! We have an intercessor in the Lord just as Peter had. (See Isaiah 59:16.)

Despite Jesus' prayer, Peter denied the Lord three times and cursed. The rooster's crow reminded Peter of Jesus' love for him. "[He] went out, and wept bitterly." A humbled repentant Peter learned not to trust his own strength. Even after the Resurrection, he almost went back to his old way of living. In John 21:3-6, he said, "I go a fishing." After a hopeless night of fishing, Jesus said, "Cast the net on the right side." After talking with Jesus later, Peter knew his fishing days were over, and he would be feeding lambs. (See John 21:15.)

Contrast Peter's denial and cursing with Judas' betrayal. Perhaps Judas wanted an earthly kingdom and thought he could push Jesus into a revolution. That would be man's way of thinking.

In Matthew 27:3-4, "Then Judas, which had betrayed him, when he saw that he was condemned, repented himself, and brought again the thirty pieces of silver to the chief priests and elders, saying, I have sinned in that I have betrayed the innocent blood. And they said, What is that to us? see thou to that." Hopeless, Judas cast down the pieces of silver in the Temple, departed, and went and hanged himself.

Judas tried to undo the betrayal. When he could not, he lost hope, and one of the twelve who had walked with Jesus ended up a suicide. Loss of hope leads to depression, doubt, and finally to suicide. Where can we go for help?

According to an article on March 4, 2003 in *The Tennessean*, "Experimental programs have demonstrated that techniques such as relaxation, group support, meditation, *even prayer*, can alter the course of some illnesses, decrease symptoms and reduce hospital stays and medication" (italics added).

We need to remember James 5:14-16. "Is any sick (depressed) among you? let him call for the elders of the church; and let them pray over him, anointing him with oil in the name of the Lord: and the prayer of faith shall save the sick, and the Lord shall raise him up; and if he have committed sins, they shall be forgiven him. Confess your faults one to another, and pray one for another, that ye may be healed. The effectual fervent prayer of a righteous man availeth much" (parentheses added).

When Grandfather J. W. Wallace, assistant pastor to Brother A. D. Gurley at the Bemis Pentecostal church, was working at the Bemis Bag Company, he was allowed time off to go pray for the sick. Mary Nell Kohlwyck Smith remembers well when she was very sick as a child and Brother Wallace came to pray for her. "I was healed instantly," she recalls. Why do we wait so long to follow God's plan?

It's true that horrible things can and often do happen when we lose hope. We must resist fear, doubt, and hopelessness. Some may ask, "What does hope mean?" Let's try to find out what hope really means.

CHAPTER 3

What Does Hope Mean?

Years ago one of the submarines of the United States sank off the coast of Massachusetts. Ships rushed to the scene. Divers dove to see if anything could be done. The sailors clung desperately to life as the oxygen supply slowly depleted. The divers and the sailors imprisoned within the submarine communicated by tapping dots and dashes of the Morse code. Time was running out and after a long pause, a question was slowly tapped out from inside the submarine: "Is . . . there . . . any . . . hope?"[1]

The agony of that question often faces every person sometime during his life.

What does hope mean? Someone once said, "Where's there's life, there's hope."

Webster's dictionary defines hope as: 1. Desire with expectation of obtaining what is desired, or belief that it is obtainable. 2. Trust; reliance. 3. Ground of source of happy expectation: hence, good promise; as a land of *hope*. 4: That which is hoped for; an object of hope.

In the book, *George W. Bush on God and Country*, President Bush said, "Hope allows us to dream big, to pray bold, and to work hard for a better future."[2]

Hope caused Abraham to leave Ur of the Chaldees because God said, "Get thee out of thy country, and from thy kindred, and from thy father's house, unto a land that I will shew thee: and I will make of thee a great nation, and I will bless thee, and make thy name great; and thou shalt be a blessing" (Genesis 12:1-2). Although Abraham never owned any of the land of Canaan except the cave of Machpelah, the tomb for him and his wife, he had a hope of a better land.

In 1492 sailors asked, "Is there a better route to India?" Hope drove Christopher Columbus as he commanded, "Sail on, sail on," although his sailors feared they would fall off the earth because they thought it was flat.

Hope of a country in which they could worship God freely according to the dictates of their own hearts drove the Puritans on the Mayflower to risk uncharted waters of the cold, stormy Atlantic. Finally they landed at Plymouth Rock, where they faced starvation and a terrible winter which left half of them dead. The rest barely survived to build this country. They left their homes in hopes of a better country.

American pioneers pushed ever westward in search of more land, a better place where they could worship God according to the dictates of their heart. Despite unfriendly natives, harsh climate, and unceasing toil, the pioneers built this great country.

Some moved west in hope of better health. Henry P. Crowell had tuberculosis, for which there was no cure in his day. On the slow train west, he stopped at a station where a grain mill was for sale. He got off the train, bought the mill, and began working. That was the beginning of Quaker Oats. Crowell made a fortune, overcame tuberculosis, and lived past the age of ninety. He discovered the meaning of health and hope.

Winston Churchill defined hope simply: "Never, never, never give up!"

A definition that I, as a garden lover, like is: "Hope is to life what seeds are to earth." Remember that the fruit is always larger and more plentiful than the seed.

Gardening, sowing seeds of hope for bright fruit and flowers for tomorrow, is a great hope builder. A *Southern Living* magazine article reported that Mrs. McHenry lives a busy life in Homewood, Alabama, balancing children and an interior design career. She declared that, "Gardening is for all ages, full of optimism and enjoyable for a lifetime. Whether it is the way you start your day or a stress reliever at the end of it, time in the garden is food for the soul." What a great definition of hope!

The symbol for hope is an anchor. Anchors stabilize us, keep us from drifting. Remember, "'Tis the set of sails and not the gales which tells us the way to go."

One writer said that the Old Testament word for hope, *tiqvah*, means a cord. This word comes from *qavah* which means "to bind together by twisting."

Hope is not defined in dollars. Tens of thousands of buyers shelled out millions of dollars to make possible a prize of $363 million in the lottery Big Game Drawing. The odds were close to seventy-six million to one. In just four days, Virginians pumped $16.5 million into the Big Game and $58 million were spent for tickets in New Jersey in 2001. Thousands were left living in a fantasy with empty pockets. Only a few won anything. The others lost all! Invest in God. He is our help. He is our hope.

The Old Testament tells us about Job. Job asked many questions. "Why died I not from the womb? why did I not give up the ghost when I came out of the belly?" (Job 3:11). He was caught between God and the devil, but he declared, "Though he slay me, yet will I trust in him" (Job 13:15).

On the cross, even Jesus questioned, "My God, my God, why hast thou forsaken me?" Nevertheless He drank the bitter cup and gave hope to all mankind. It was a dark Friday, but He knew Sunday was coming! When we have hard questions, we must keep on "keeping on" knowing that an answer is on the way.

Before Lloyd Ogilvie wrote the book *A Future and a Hope*, he severely injured himself in a fall on an isolated beachfront area one stormy night. But he kept pushing and dragging himself, holding on to hope. Later he was able to say, "The Lord spared my life, healed me and gave me a new beginning! I had to find Him in pain." Ogilvie held on to hope.[3]

Nancy Guthrie, who lost two babies to an incurable disease, found comfort in Luke 9:23-25 in *The Message*, "Anyone who intends to come with me has to let me lead. You're not in the driver's seat—I am. Don't run from suffering; embrace it. Follow me and I'll show you how. Self-help is no help at all. Self-sacrifice is the way, my way, to finding yourself, your true self. What good would it do to

get everything you want and lose you, the real you?"[4]
Learn from suffering.

Hope Makes a Difference:
Hope opens doors where despair closes them.
Hope draws its power from deeply trusting God
    and what He does to change people's lives.
Hope lights a candle instead of "cursing the
    darkness."
Hope regards problems, small or large, as
    opportunities.
Hope cherishes no illusions, but it does not yield
    to cynicism or despair.

(Author Unknown)

It's possible to put our hopes in wrong places. I
worked with a woman who had a doctorate degree in
medical history, but she was working as a file clerk at
Peabody College for Teachers. She failed to ask if there
were many job opportunities in medical history. If you
cannot make a living using the gifts God has given you,
find a job to earn a living. Then make your gifts and tal-
ents your hobby.

Our daughter, Rosemary, is a gifted artist, but she
could not find a job in art where she lived in a small
Mississippi town. I wrote the department of labor and
asked, "Where are the job opportunities in Mississippi?"
They answered: computer and health care. Her pastor
had two daughters: one with a two-year degree in nursing who found a good job; the other had a bachelor's in
music but only taught in her father's small church
school. So Rosemary graduated *cum laude* in nursing

and has a great job in that field today. Her art is her hobby. When she retires, she will have an interesting purpose for her days.

People, young or old, without purpose—a goal, do not know how to define hope. Robert Fulghum once worked as a hotel night clerk. His food was furnished, but the cost was deducted from his pay. For a few days, he was served two hot dogs and sauerkraut. He complained bitterly and threatened to quit. His co-worker, a quiet Jew who had survived Auschwitz, listened for a while, then said, "Fulghum, you need to learn the difference between inconvenience and a problem. There is a difference between a lump in the oatmeal, a lump in your throat and a lump in your breast."

The health industry is a leading business in America. We have conquered smallpox, polio, and other killers, but we still have heart disease, strokes, and cancer. One of the major causes of some of these problems appears to be stress which leads to loss of hope.

Although multitudes followed Jesus with a myriad of health problems, hunger and thirst, He felt compassion and touched them, but occasionally even He withdrew for a time of quiet and prayer.

Prevention magazine listed six ways to combat stress: take a break, tune it out, take a walk, write it out, customize your work space and/or take a pill. I prefer to walk through our garden. My work space is here in the sunroom which my son, Jeff, built. Tall trees filled with singing birds surround me. Great stress busters!

David skillfully played on his harp to soothe the stressed-out King Saul. We can find meaning and hope as we sing old hymns, praise and worship music, and/or contemporary gospel music to drive away the doubts and depression that cloud our days. It's great to live in Music City, USA! Music helps us to hope.

The beloved, blind, sweet singer, Fanny Crosby, who wrote over two thousand hymns, lost her sight at a young age due to the wrong medicine. She did not learn to write her name until she was old. Friends copied the words to her wonderful hymns. She was paid very little, but she held on to hope. Her songs help us to find the meaning of hope. They still bring hope to hungry hearts. Fanny Crosby knew the definition of hope.

A contemporary children's writer, Judith Viorst, wrote a book about the problems children face. She titled the book, *Alexander and the Terrible, Horrible, No Good, Very Bad Day*. An adult can have days like that! You overslept. Your best suit needed pressing and there was a button off the blouse. Then when you put on your last pair of hose, they popped a runner. A hopeless day! Don't let such a start ruin your whole day. Try singing that old song, "Zippity Do Dah! My oh My What a Wonderful Day." Don't take a day off and lay on the couch.

Inactivity steals hope. After his terrible accident, Lloyd Ogilvie couldn't pastor, preach, or produce radio programs. All he could do was read his Bible, pray, rest, and enjoy being alive. The Lord told him, "I love you not for what you *do*, but for what you are—My person."[5]

In preparing notes for this book, I read and studied while at our favorite vacation spot, St. George Island, off the coast of Florida on the Gulf of Mexico. In November only a few people come here so we enjoy the privacy and quiet far from crowded tourist places.

During a storm one night, two houses down from our

place, a boat about seventy feet long washed ashore. The owner said his motor conked out and he couldn't restart it.

The boat rocked back and forth crazily during windy days. It tipped way over, useless. The owner hoped a high tide would get his boat afloat. A man on a bulldozer came and dug around it. After a hard rain, the owner got a pump to empty water out of the vessel. People came, stared and talked about the problem. Some said if it wasn't rescued, it could legally become salvage property. Was it a hopeless situation?

Finally one day a shrimp ship came steaming up along with a smaller boat. After several tries, they finally got a rope aboard and eventually secured the ship. The shrimper, along with the smaller ship, began to carefully move on out. Soon the beached boat was afloat. What seemed to be a hopeless situation ended well. But this is not always the case.

One man said, "I don't pray for calmer seas; I ask God for a stronger ship." Remember the Titanic was built by experts who vowed that it was unsinkable. Noah, an amateur who had never seen rain, built the ark according to God's blueprint.

Boredom can lead to loss of hope. "You can have a great time partying," the devil promises a life of pleasure. Who needs grandmother's God? Even God's own people can lose hope and get caught in the enemy's snares. Remember Moses and the children of Israel.

When Moses went up the mountain to pray, the people got bored. "Make us a god, Aaron. We don't know what's happened to Moses." So spineless Aaron gathered their wealth, their gold and made them a god.

When Moses and Joshua came down from Mount

Sinai, they heard the boisterous party. Angrily Moses dealt with the problem, ground up their god of gold, and made them drink it. Aaron stuttered around saying, "You know how these people are, Moses. I just took their gold, threw it in the fire and this god came out." Had it not been for Moses' complete devotion to his people, God may have destroyed them as He threatened.

People still try to make homemade gods. The devil is alive and well and in the party business today. Too many Aarons try to make gods. Many foolish souls follow false leaders. Hundreds followed Jim Jones and obediently drank poison Kool-aid, thinking Jones could give them hope, convinced that he was a man of God.

Bored people fall prey to the siren call of today's pleasure-oriented world. But today's parties often end with lung cancer, AIDS, unwanted pregnancies, broken lives, and loss of hope.

Remember we are not promised Easy Street. Life's pathway is often strewn with storms: financial disaster, an unhealthy newborn, and an unexpected diagnosis of a brain tumor. A sudden car wreck totaled the car of an elderly couple, dooming them to dependence on friends and relatives. They found hope when their caring daughter sold her home and bought a large home in order to take care of them. Now they can still go to church and find hope in Him.

Sometimes tornadoes destroy churches as well as homes. An abusive husband destroyed the trust of his children and love of his wife. A young man speeding through a red light crashed into a senior on her way to church. Christians are certainly subject to the vicissitudes of life. So the list goes on. Just read the church's prayer list or the daily paper.

Where do you turn when you are faced with broken dreams, divorce, financial disaster, diseases that lead to death?

Job's wife said, "Just curse God and die." Others take out their anger on their loved ones. Some live in denial and never face their problems, hoping they will go away. One writer said, "Denial blindfolds pain and blocks the path to progress." These approaches do not lead to lasting healing and hope. Norman Cousins said, "Drugs are not always necessary, but belief in recovery always is."

A Chinese proverb defines hope like this, "The longest journey starts with the first step." It may be steps up a steep mountain, but hope will keep us climbing. To know the way up the mountain, ask the One who made the mountain. Your mountain path may be strewn with sharp rocks, leaving bloody footprints. We know that it is a narrow path and few there be that find it. But this path named *hope* is the only road upward. The broad way leads down to destruction.

So experience builds our hope—not in ourselves—but in the One who made the mountain and the paths up it. Isaiah said, "For my thoughts are not your thoughts, neither are your ways my ways, saith the LORD. For as the heavens are higher than the earth, so are my ways higher than your ways, and my thoughts than your thoughts" (Isaiah 55:8-9).

Paul quoted Isaiah in I Corinthians 2:9: "Eye hath not seen, nor ear heard, neither have entered into the heart of man, the things which God hath prepared for them that love him." What a blessed definition of hope!

Now that we have defined hope, the next question is: "Is there any hope? Where do we go to find hope?"

52

CHAPTER 4

Is There Any Hope?

John 5:3 records the story of a crippled man who had hope deferred. In Jerusalem, by the sheep gate, a pool called Bethesda offered a limited supply of hope. Many hopeless people: blind, crippled, helpless, friendless, gathered at the pool every day awaiting an angel to come down and trouble the water. They believed that the first person who stepped into the pool after the water was troubled would be made well of whatever disease he had. Often a certain man came who had suffered from an infirmity for thirty-eight years. Thirty-eight long years he had wondered, "Is there any hope for me? Will anyone ever help me to be the first one in the pool? Is there any hope?"

Then one day Jesus came. He always seems to come where there are needy, helpless people. He sought out the most needy, the man who had been there for thirty-eight years. Certainly that crippled man had his hope deferred! Bethesda pool offered his only hope, but Jesus came and met his need more than an angel ever could.

The December 2002 issue of *Ladies' Home Journal* carried a touching story of hope deferred. About 11:15 on a warm July evening, a mother from southwestern Pennsylvania called her daughter to tell her that her father and husband were in a mining accident. Within seconds a state police officer made the nightmare official. Eighteen men on the three-to-eleven shift had been involved in a freak accident underground. Only nine had made it to safety. Then came the dreadful news; the men had accidentally pierced a wall into an abandoned adjoining mine that was flooded with water. This unleashed a fifty-million-gallon torrent into Quecreek. When the miners' families heard this, they almost lost hope. Many of them knew about the shafts and tunnels of the mines. They knew that the water would more than fill Quecreek. They could visualize their loved ones floating together, lifeless. Friends and families gathered and prayed all through the night, clinging together for hope. Rescuers drilled a six-inch-wide hole to pump in warm air. At 5:30 A.M., they heard tapping on the drill. This rekindled hope.

Two days went by. The water continued to rise. The rescuers decided to send an air generator down the small hole and seal it. This would provide oxygen to the men and force water out of the tunnels, but it cut off further communication.

Is There Any Hope?

On Thursday afternoon, the rescue teams had received a thirty-inch drilling rig, hoping to carve an escape hole wide enough to allow a metal basket to be lowered to bring up the miners. About 2 A.M. the drill bit broke off halfway down the escape tunnel, causing a delay of at least nineteen hours.

New equipment arrived at noon Friday, and the rescuers began boring a second escape shaft. The miners had not been heard from for forty-eight hours.

They battled the powerful gusher of water, first crawling along with the current while holding on to the coal conveyor belt, trying to find an escape route, then crawling back in search of higher ground. They found an eighteen-by-sixty-foot shelf dry but too rocky to sit or lie down comfortably. The men prayed. They took turns sharing a pen, scribbling last words onto scraps of cardboard, then sealing them in the lunch bucket. One man suggested that they bind themselves together by slipping a metal cable through their belt loops so they would not be separated.

When the rescuers finally reached the miners at 10:15 Saturday evening, the men didn't hear it because of the noise of the generator. Then they saw the hole! Food, water, and a phone were dropped down. They were rescued shortly afterward. From Wednesday night until Saturday noon, the miners and their rescuers lived in an almost hopeless situation. They often asked, "Is there any hope?" Then all nine miners were rescued! After the rescue, the miners told that a lunch bucket with a perfectly dry corned beef sandwich and a soda floated right up to the ravished men. Coincidence? They didn't think so.[1] Deborah Mathis, columnist for *The Tennesseean* wrote, "There was an Unseen Mover in The Miracle of the Mine!"

Hosea 2:15 speaks of the "valley of Achor for a door of hope." Have you thought you had a door open only to have it slam in your face? Wait, I say, wait on God. The crippled man waited thirty-eight years. The miners waited for three days.

In II Corinthians 11:24-30, Paul listed his trials: beatings, stonings, shipwrecks, perils of water, robbers, his own countrymen, the heathen. Perils in the city, perils in the wilderness, perils in the sea, perils among false brethren, weariness, painfulness, hunger and thirst, cold and nakedness! You name it! Paul met giants of trouble everywhere he went. But he suffered through trials and triumphantly declared that he *gloried* in it!

Then Paul further declared in Romans 8:28, "And we know that all things work together for good to them that love God, to them who are the called according to his purpose." Not all things that happen *are* good, but they work together for good. A firm basis for hope! A lot of things that happen are certainly not good, but keep on loving God and serving Him and life will work out well. This kind of hope is saving hope. Read Romans 5:3-4, "But we *glory* in tribulations also: knowing that tribulation worketh patience; and patience, experience; and experience, *hope*" (italics added). As the song says, "If we never had a problem, we wouldn't know that God could solve them." So just sit a moment and begin to count your blessings and hope will build.

However, not every sorrow always turns into a blessing. Not every storm brings a rainbow. Tornadoes ripped through Tennessee leaving death and destruction. My brother-in-law's home was somewhat damaged and our district superintendent's home had its roof blown off. My daughter said that same night two tornadoes roared through Columbus, Mississippi, their old hometown. The downtown area which had been hit by tornadoes before was again damaged.

Later tornadoes again hit Jackson, Tennessee. The morning news said that downtown Jackson looked like a war zone. Seven people were killed. That same night a tornado hit Kansas City, killing fifteen. It also ripped through my hometown, Finley, Tennessee, felling many of the trees and blowing off the steeple of the Pentecostal church.

Certainly we do face storms in life. Often we ask, "Is there any hope?" Earlier our minister preached on storms that we face. He used Mark 4:35-39. In chapter 3, Jesus had healed the man with the withered hand as well as many others. Then He asked for a small ship, and He taught the parable of the seed to the twelve. Later He taught the parable of the sower from the ship. He said, "Let us pass over unto the other side" (Mark 4:35). Then He went into the hinder part of the ship for a much needed rest.

Soon a great storm of wind and waves began to beat into the ship. Immediately the disciples doubted that Jesus even cared for them. They had forgotten that He had said, "Let us pass *over* to the other side." Storm clouds, high winds and waves threatened them. They had seen withered hands restored, but wind and waves were something else. Jesus arose from sleep, rebuked the wind, and said unto the sea, "Peace, be still." "The wind ceased, and there was a great calm." Then Jesus asked, "Why are ye so fearful? how is it that ye have no faith?" Apparently this frightened the apostles even more. One said to another, "What manner of man is this, that even the wind and the sea obey him?" Hope helps us to remember the God of the storm who can carry us through storms to the other side!

Read Moffatt's translation in Romans 10:11, "No one who believes in him will ever be disappointed . . . No one." Isaiah advised, "They that wait upon the LORD shall renew their strength" (Isaiah 40:31). (See also Isaiah 8:17.)

In John 9:2, the disciples asked Jesus, "Why is this man blind? Who sinned?" Paul spoke of our light affliction, which is but for a moment (II Corinthians 4:17).

It is hard not to question when God is so silent. Sometimes the circumstance that causes us the most pain and confusion is not what God says to us, but the fact that in the midst of difficulty, He seems to say nothing at all. Job wanted answers. "Why all this pain and suffering? Let the Almighty answer me" (paraphrase added) (Job 31:35). Finally God did answer. Read Job's reply, Job 40:1-5. Sometimes dreams die. All hope seems lost. We ask, "Is there any hope?" Ever felt that way?

Suffering is a mystery, and Job respected that mystery. Because he knew who God is, he could accept what God gave even when he didn't understand. Job had no idea how much his faithfulness in such extreme difficulty mattered. But it did. Now thousands of years later, we learn from the wonderful account of Job's suffering.

Extreme difficulty matters so much. Our response to testing matters, too. We don't have to understand, but we do have to remain obedient. Can you choose to trust God and continue believing He has a plan and a purpose, even though you don't understand it?

We find ourselves hunting for answers, searching for help and hope. Sometimes a close friend who just listens helps us to keep hoping. "A true and genuine friend, one of those very few special persons who enter my life, is one with whom I can share my brokenness without feeling challenged," said one renewed clergyman.

Friends help us hold on to a seed of hope. In her book, *A Life for a Life*, published in 1860, Dinah Maria Muloch Craik wrote a beautiful paragraph on the blessings of friendship. "But, oh the blessing it is to have a friend to whom one can speak fearlessly on any subject, with whom one's deepest as well as one's most foolish thoughts come out simply and safely. Oh, the comfort—the inexpressible comfort of feeling safe with a person—having neither to weigh thoughts nor measure words, but pouring them all right out, just as they are, chaff and grain together, certain that a faithful hand will take and sift them, keep what is worth keeping, and then with the breath of kindness blow the rest away."

John Donne said it well, "No man is an island, entire of itself; every man is a piece of the continent, a part of the main." Hold on to family, church, and friends. They plant seeds of hope.

> It was only a sunny smile, and little it cost in the
> giving.
> But like the morning light, it scattered the night,
> and made the day worth living.
>   (Anonymous Author)

Hope is hard work. I had an aunt who was so badly abused that she fled in the night. Many years later at her death, a relative said Aunt Faye never spoke a bad thing. She held on to hope. Trouble only made her better, not bitter.

On D-Day, Dwight Eisenhower's order of the day was "Let us all beseech the blessing of Almighty God upon this great and noble undertaking." General Eisenhower knew that only faith in God could help these men hold on to hope!

Loneliness causes people to lose hope. Today's world is full of lonely people. Broken homes and hearts, disease-wracked bodies, disturbed, depressed minds cause us to lose hold on hope. We ask, "Is there any hope?"

When my mother died suddenly of a heart attack, on her piano lay a sheet of music entitled "Learning to Lean." The last time she sang in the choir, they sang, "Soon and very soon, we are going to see the King." Until her last few days, Mom was learning to lean on Jesus. He is our hope. Each new day, we must learn again to lean on Him.

Statistics tell us that 156,000 Christian martyrs died in 1994, and there have been many more since the trouble in the Mideast. AIDS is making Africa a continent of orphans, themselves also often carriers of the HIV virus. What will our grandchildren face in a few years? How important it is to teach them to lean on Jesus, who is our hope.

Today I received an e-mail telling about two young women working in an orphanage in Haiti. The island is in a terrible uproar. Americans are urged to flee the country, but these two young girls are determined to stay with the thirty children that they are responsible for. They hold on to hope in a dangerous and almost hopeless situation.

Many children do not have the privilege of a godly upbringing. A friend of mine, Brian Stewart, grew up in a very bad neighborhood of run-down homes. Here is his story.

"I was exposed to things no child should have to see or hear. I saw grown people having sex on the porch while my friends and I, who were about eleven or twelve years old, played together on the porch next to them.

"I also witnessed grown men beating their elderly father half to death on the same porch. My friends and I played out front while police cars parked nearby. The people next door being arrested for drugs and violence did not faze us. I was also exposed to pornography at the young age of five or six. Little did I know how drastically my adult life would be affected by my childhood, which leads me to my testimony.

"The effects of my childhood started to surface during the time I was dating the girl who would become not only my wife but also the single best thing to happen in my life next to my salvation and having a relationship with the Lord.

"We were married in 1979. She was fifteen and I was eighteen. She had no idea at the time of what was manifesting itself inside of me. It started with a mild curiosity in pornography and slowly grew over the next six months into a habit or hobby or whatever you want to call it. I thought I had it under control, when without warning, the enemy whom I had no idea was controlling me, shifted into high gear. I started getting into extremely hard-core porn movies, books, magazines, etc. I also started to abuse my wife verbally. I made sick demands on her that she refused to cooperate with. This made me angrier every day. The pornography started to consume my every thought. I threatened my wife when she refused to do what I asked her to do. My once 'hobby' had become a full-blown addiction. I reached a point where the sickest, most depraved things became not only acceptable, but also exciting and expected.

"At that time, I cared more about the addiction than I

did my wife or daughter. I put her through things that would cause most women to leave or kill their husbands. The more I degraded her, the better I felt about myself. It didn't bother me at all that she was starting to hate herself. I was dragging her down with me, and it didn't matter at all to me. Yet somehow, in the midst of my threats and sick demands, she managed to pray for me. She loved me and believed that some day God would bring out the good man hidden deep inside of me. On the other hand, I wanted no part of God or the good man in me.

"I continued to get worse and worse, coming to the point where pornography was no longer a part of my life, I was part of it. It consumed me. I no longer knew who I was. I had no identity, no concern over whether I lived or died. After about eleven and a half years, when I thought things could not possibly get worse, they did.

"On top of this life-consuming obsession, I developed severe panic and anxiety attacks, only to be followed shortly thereafter by something called sleep apnea. All of this threw me into deep depression. This lasted an additional three and a half years, during which time I contemplated suicide twice. Death for me was a viable option. Over the course of fourteen years, I went from loving life to praying for death literally. I started to work part-time at my church in the maintenance department. At age thirty-two, I hit rock bottom with nowhere to look, but up.

"One day shortly thereafter, a missionary who was visiting the church saw me standing in the foyer. I must have looked very lost because he walked up to me and said that the Lord had told him that I needed prayer. 'May I pray for you?' he asked. At that point, I had never had anyone but my wife pray for me.

"Instead of being nervous, I responded, 'PLEASE!' As he prayed, I felt a release, as though a ton of bricks was taken off my back. The HOPE that I thought was lost forever started to return.

"The very next morning I gave my life to the Lord, and the fourteen-year-long prayer of my wife was answered. In a split second, God delivered me from pornography, panic, anxiety, sleep apnea, depression, and thoughts of suicide. I gave it all to Him, and He took it all away right then and there. I have been a Christian now serving and loving and living for the Lord for ten years, without any of the old sickness. How dare I not serve a God who would do all this for someone like me."

In a horrible situation, Brian found a seed of hope. Others in almost hopeless circumstances ask, "Where do I go for help and hope?"

CHAPTER 5

Where Do We Go to Find Hope?

"We give thanks to God and the Father of our Lord Jesus Christ, praying always for you, since we heard of your faith in Christ Jesus, and of the love which ye have to all the saints, for the *hope* which is laid up for you in heaven" (italics added) (Colossians 1:3-5).

Where do we go to find this blessed hope?

There is hope! That is God's message to the world. The apostles believed it. David proclaimed it. David said God knew him before he was born. "But thou art he that took me out of the womb: thou didst make me hope when I was upon my mother's breasts" (Psalm 22:9). In Psalm 71:5, David said, "For thou art my *hope*, O Lord GOD:

thou art my trust from my youth" (italics added). Few people are pursued by insane kings as David was. But whether it was lions, bears, giants, insane kings, or his own rebellious son, David from his youth knew where to go for help and hope.

He reminded us to call to remembrance all the goodness of God. "Remember the past, don't forget His works and keep His commandments." Again in Psalm 42:5, David asked himself: "Why art thou cast down, O my soul? and why art thou disquieted in me? *hope* thou in God: for I shall yet praise him for the help of his countenance" (italics added).

Memory helps us sow seeds of hope. In I Samuel 7:12, the children of Israel at Samuel's command gathered at Mizpeh, where Samuel set up a stone of remembrance and called the name of it Ebenezer saying, "Hitherto hath the LORD helped us." Remembering what God has done in the past will renew hope.

Peter once doubted, denied, and ran from a small servant girl. After Calvary Peter was so discouraged, devastated, and full of doubt that he let the women go alone to the tomb. But once he got his Pentecostal blessing, doubts and fears left him. He wrote to the dispersed Jews in his first letter: "Blessed be the God and Father of our Lord Jesus Christ, which according to his abundant mercy hath begotten us again unto a lively hope by the resurrection of Jesus Christ from the dead" (I Peter 1:3). Peter certainly knew about the Lord's mercy. Now he had not just hope, but *lively* hope. As Paul is known as the apostle of faith and John as the apostle of love, so Peter is known as the apostle of hope.

Luke 24:13 tells us about two doubting, disillusioned,

and depressed disciples who walked away from Jerusalem with their hopes shattered. "What are you talking about?" Jesus asked as He joined them.

Cleopas answered saying, "Are you a stranger in Jerusalem? Don't you know what's happened?"

"What things?" Jesus asked.

"They crucified Jesus, a prophet mighty before God and all the people. We had hoped that He was the Messiah who would redeem Israel. All this happened three days ago. Some of the women were astonished when they went to His sepulcher and could not find Him. They said they saw an angel which said He was alive. Some of His followers went but Him they saw not."

"O fools, and slow of heart to believe all that the prophets have spoken: Ought not Christ to have suffered these things, and to enter into his glory?" Jesus explained the Crucifixion and the Resurrection going all the way back to Moses and the prophets.

As they drew nigh their village, they begged Jesus to abide with them saying, "It's evening and the day is far spent." He went with them to eat and took bread and blessed it and gave to them.

Finally their eyes were opened and they realized who their traveling Friend was, but Jesus vanished out of their sight. Then they said, "Did not our heart burn within us?" With newfound faith and hope they returned to Jerusalem saying, "He is risen indeed!"

The road is much brighter when we go back to Jerusalem. When we walk with Jesus, there are always seeds of hope. Friday is dark, but Sunday's coming! In times of deep disappointment, doubt, despair, and defeat, turn to the Scriptures. There you will meet Jesus and find hope.

Matthew 18:19 spelled hope for me. In 1942 my sweetheart had been in the army since 1941. When he asked me to marry him, I asked him to agree with me, relying on this scripture, that he would not have to go overseas in World War II. Only eighteen I was scared of the danger he would face on the European battlefield. So we agreed as that scripture says, "If two of you shall agree on earth as touching any thing that they shall ask, it shall be done for them of my Father which is in heaven." My husband, J. O., served in the army for four years and four months and was at the embarkation port when VE day was declared. That was our Ebenezer! A direct answer to prayer! I still turn to Matthew 18:19 to find seeds of hope in time of trouble.

I love to read biographies of great men and women. As a writer, although I wrote dozens of fictional stories for young children, when I began to write for adults, I chose biographies rather than fiction. Real stories about real people who have lived and taught and preached the gospel of Jesus Christ. I especially enjoyed compiling stories of our early Pentecostal pioneers. Faith and hope rise as we read how these men and women survived famines, floods, financial disasters, storms, poor health, hurts, humiliations, depression, and doubts. They faced it all. We can go to history to find hope.

My cousin, Patsy McGinnis, took my brothers, my sister, and me over a rutted hillside, through brambles, briers, thorns, and thickets to a neglected cemetery in the hills above Finley, my hometown. Although my grandmother had taken us on jaunts in those hills as children, I don't remember ever before seeing the tall tombstone of my great-grandfather, Eli S. Hardwick. He was a Methodist preacher and father of several sons and daughters. As I stood by his tombstone, I wondered what stories he could have told. What troubles and trials did he face? Where did he go for hope?

Patsy told us of going through a pasture with a bull in it outside Corinth, Mississippi. She scrambled over a rusty barbed wire fence. Her guide cautioned, "Watch out for rattlesnakes! Be careful about stepping in the poison ivy." Finally in a grove of pines, she found the tombstone of Eli's father, Liberty Hardwick, our great-great-grandfather. Liberty was a Baptist preacher who had deeded land for a church and a cemetery. The church burned, and the members decided to rebuild in another place. What prayers had Liberty prayed? How had he felt God? In planning for the church and cemetery, he must have thought he was planting seeds of hope for the future. Dozens of his descendants are scattered throughout the United States. Where did Liberty go for hope?

Some say the famous painting by Jean Francois Millet, *Man with Hoe*, represents the dignity of labor. Others think it only shows a man crushed and almost defeated. If one adds only one letter to the word, *Hoe*, he spells *Hope*. One letter makes all the difference. Perhaps many a man with a hoe has been almost crushed. Poor tools, hard rocky soil, no rain can make a farmer's life seem hopeless. Others work with what they have, even if it's only a hoe.

Every man and woman needs a hoe, a pencil or a computer, something to do, a purpose. My grandmother fought nut grass with a hoe and helped her blind son with his vegetable garden. She lived for more than eighty years. A hoe is not a hopeless tool. In the hands of a willing worker, a hoe can plant a beautiful garden! My husband, with his tiller and a hoe and the sweat of his brow, reaps a fine harvest of tomatoes, peppers, okra, and other vegetables which we all enjoy. Recently he planted a perennial garden for us to enjoy beautiful flowers as well as food.

Some look at the gorgeous seed catalogs. Some may even buy seed. But a true gardener began work last year, had the soil tested, perhaps added some potassium, fertilizer, then got lime, broadcast it, made detailed plans, ordered seed, tilled the land, laid out rows, then sharpened his hoe. Hard work, a hoe, and hope can go hand in hand and plant seeds of hope for a harvest. Will Rogers said, "What this country needs is more dirty fingernails!" Calloused hands, dirty nails, hard work, then God's sunshine and rain in right proportions bring a harvest. But you can't grow a garden while sitting in the shade singing, "Oh, How Beautiful!"

Work is honorable and healthy and builds hope. Today's affluence robs our children of the need to help and thereby creates boredom which leads to all sorts of problems, even crime.

A hoe must not only be in the hand of a willing worker, but also a wise worker lest his will to work will be defeated and hopeless. Roethke said, "In a dark time the eye begins to see." Proverbs 10:5 tells about a wise son, "He that gathereth in summer is a wise son: but he that sleepeth in harvest is a son that causeth shame." All honest labor is dignified. God provides a robin with food, but He doesn't throw the worms in the nest.

A Chinese man whose name was Lo became a Christian and was reading the New Testament for the first time. When he got to the last verse in Matthew, he became very excited. He told a friend, "The Lord Jesus wrote this for me because He said, 'Lo, I am with you always.'" And Lo was correct. The Lord was speaking to him and to each and every one of us.[1]

We can go to friends to find hope. Hold on to true friends, even those who just come to hold your hand. Try to forgive Job's comforters who come to point fingers, pontificate, and probe. One minister said, "Bitterness is like a rattlesnake. If you grab it by the tail, it will bite you." Bitterness also leads to brittleness, which is easily broken. Remember Jesus came to heal the broken hearted.

Some of us were blessed and could turn to parents to find hope. Jesus said, "Or what man is there of you, whom if his son ask bread, will he give him a stone? Or if he ask a fish, will he give him a serpent? If ye then, being evil, know how to give good gifts unto your children, how much more shall your Father which is in heaven give good things to them that ask him?" (Matthew 7:9-11).

Faith and love grow in the seeds of hope. Hope is laid up in heaven. In a prison cell in Rome, Paul wrote to encourage the saints in Colosse (Colossians 1:3-5).

Hope helps us establish memorials. As early as the days of Abraham, believers buried their dead. They established memorials. I stood in awe when we visited Abraham's tomb in Hebron. Sister Ruby Martin taught us in Bible school that there were ten generations from Adam to Noah, ten generations from Noah to Abraham. And here I was standing at Abraham's tomb. His DNA is probably found in Jewish descendants today.

Dr. Charles Rohlen, a retired college professor, traced our genealogy back to 1000. He traced Grandmother Hardwick's family, the Joslins, back to

France in 900. Old European churches kept good records. Jewish people are very interested in genealogy. Matthew and Mark record the line of Jesus. Although His parents were from Nazareth (Can there any good thing come out of Nazareth?) (see John 1:46), Jesus could trace His genealogy back to King David. Today Jewish people scattered to the four corners of the earth find seeds of hope in their connection to King David. Their finest hotel in Jerusalem is called the King David Hotel.

Family stories passed down from generation to generation plant seeds of hope, or they may hinder. Grandfather Wallace's father left his family when he was only twelve. Although he was very young, J. W. Wallace took responsibility for his mother, two sisters, and two younger brothers. He became a lay minister in the Methodist church, then accepted Pentecost. Later he felt his call to preach! After he was fifty, he left a good job and the pastorate of a great church, moved to Nashville and established the first Pentecostal church east of the Tennessee River. Later with his son, J. O., my husband, they bought a church building in Goodlettsville, Tennessee. My husband pastored it while still in the army. It is a thriving church today. Now more than seventy-two churches are planted east of the Tennessee River!

After my husband was discharged from the army, he went to Bob Jones College on the GI Bill of Rights, taught Bible school in Tupelo, Mississippi, for a year, then he and Papa Wallace bought another church in south Nashville and established the Woodbine Pentecostal church. Papa Wallace had hope for the future. A vision of not just one church east of the Tennessee River but one in each part of Nashville as well as further east. He left his church in West

Nashville (now called First United Pentecostal Church) with his assistant, went on to Oak Ridge, met with a small group, bought great property on the main street in town. In the late fifties, my husband pastored there.

Papa Wallace did not let neglect by his father hinder him. He was not a victim but a victor! As a twelve-year-old, he picked up the load and carried the responsibility of a father, a pastor, a church builder—a man of vision and hope. What great family stories to hand down. Rather than blame abusive parents and curse the darkness, light a candle. Break the generational curse!

Great family stories inspire hope! Elie Wiesel said, "God made men because He loves stories." However poorly written, family stories, diaries, and letters plant seeds of hope. "Were I to await perfection, my book would never be written," one writer commented.

I gathered a lot of material for my book, *It's Real,* about Clarence Nelson from simple little diaries that his wife had kept for years. My son-in-law, Jerry McNall, was so happy to get his mother's diaries that she had kept for many years. One writer said, "All of our theology must eventually become biography."

Tim Hansel in his book, *You Gotta Keep Dancin',* told how he was paralyzed in his own pain, cynicism. "I feel so inept, so weak, so ugly, that I want to shun even myself . . . More bad news. I've realized more strongly than ever that you don't truly discover your roots until you are at the bottom of the pit. From this perspective you are no longer distracted by usual superficialities . . . I looked up the word 'root.' It means 'to dig down in some mass in order to find something valuable.' . . . God is teaching me through all this to rediscover the substance of my strength and my song. Perhaps this is an unusual opportunity to discover who I really am."[2]

Hope sets goals. In the forties, Golda Meier came to New York in a print dress with only ten dollars in her pocket. She left with thousands of dollars promised to help arm Israel in their first fight to secure their homeland. Golda had a hope and a goal for Israel.

Several years ago, some friends wanted to go to Israel with a church choir. They left with only five dollars spending money, told no one, but friends began to buy souvenirs for them and hand them money. Were they risk takers? Sure they were. But they have wonderful memories not only of a great trip, but also of great friends.

We strengthen our hopes when we set goals. Some seniors have set a goal to further educate themselves and begin to study with hope. I read an inspiring story about a Jewish senior who applied to Harvard for a scholarship to study geriatrics. He got the scholarship. Now why couldn't I have thought of that!

When we visited in northeast India back in the seventies, some new friends of mine gave me a gift of hand-woven dark blue cotton. They explained that this was a "no-step-back cloth!" When warriors of that area went to war, they wore this cloth. This meant they were in the battle until they won or died trying. These were warriors with purpose, courage, conviction, and hope.

When I was sixteen, my grandmother made me a homemade hope chest. In those days, young girls began embroidering linen and collecting things for the home they hoped to have. That chest traveled with me to California, where I married my soldier boyfriend. For three years, that chest went with us on all our army moves. Then it was with us on all our moves in the ministry. My homemade hope chest today has a place of honor in my home.

The First United Pentecostal Church of Nashville presents a play called *Azusa Street*. It tells the story of the black minister, Brother Seymour, from Texas who was invited to come to Los Angeles to preach about the Holy Spirit. When he preached about speaking in an unknown tongue, the pastor refused to let him continue. Friends on Bonnie Brae Street opened their home. The house filled and the crowd overflowed to the front porch. The porch gave way and caved in. Finally they secured a former church on Azusa Street. There the Lord poured out the Holy Spirit so freely that Frank Bartleman from one of the newspapers came to investigate this phenomena. Bartleman came to write a new story, but God filled him with the Holy Spirit. He wrote a book about that great meeting, which is still in print today. Bartleman received that blessed hope, and the revival spread all over the United States. Now it has spread all over the world, and Pentecostalism is one of the fastest growing religious movements of the twenty-first century.

In Acts 2:38, we read where the disciples, who had been so hopeless at the Crucifixion, regained hope at the Resurrection and received power on the Day of Pentecost.

"It is impossible to enslave, mentally or socially, a Bible reading people. The principles of the Bible are the groundwork of human freedom," said Horace Greeley. *The New York Times* lists current bestsellers, but we should always remember that the all-time bestselling book published today is the Bible. It has been for years. No other book comes close to having been read, reread, owned, and cherished by more people. Many different versions, translations, and editions of the Bible are printed every year. There is no way to calculate how many Bibles have been published through the years here in America. Plus we send thousands overseas. Missionaries have translated the Bible into almost every tongue under heaven. It is not a mark of intelligence or well-rounded education to ignore the Bible even though today's politically correct crowd reject God's Word. They try to ignore the fact that man was made a spiritual being in His image.

In his book, *The American Leadership Tradition*, Marvin Olasky tells us that General George Washington knew his Bible and carried out church duties as a vestryman from 1762 onward. According to one of his grandsons, Washington's wife, Martha, read from the Bible and prayed an hour each morning. General Schwarzkopf read his Bible every night during the Desert Storm conflict.

One of the most interesting Bibles I have ever owned just came to us recently. It is the Joslin family Bible dating back to 1800 and containing the family records of Rosa Belle Joslin Hardwick, my paternal grandmother.

Pioneers carried Bibles across this country in covered wagons and read them by candlelight. Viktor Frankl said, "The only thing we can leave for posterity is what we put into the next generation." So our forefathers read their Bibles and found seeds of hope. Many came to this country with only a dream, but hardship strengthened them and they found hope in Him.

Once a little boy stuck his hand in a bottle to retrieve a penny at the bottom. His hand stuck in the narrow neck of the bottle. "Straighten your fingers," his father said. "I can't," answered the little boy. "I'll lose my penny."

We need to let go the little things that keep us trapped in bottles of our own making and trust God for the big things in our lives. Victor Hugo said it well, "Have courage for the great trials of life and patience for the small ones, and when you have laboriously completed your daily tasks, lie down to sleep. God is awake!"

The Serenity Prayer says it another way, "God, grant me the serenity to accept the things I cannot change; courage to change the things I can; and wisdom to know the difference." Don't hold to old painful bitter memories. Let go and find hope for a better tomorrow.

Find hope in the gospel of the Lord Jesus Christ. Hope in God, said all the apostolic messengers. The prophets of old electrified people with the same good news.

For seventy years, the Communists in Russia tried to eliminate God, but one day the wall came tumbling down. I read a story about a publisher who was allowed to carry in some Bibles for display. They were quickly snatched up. One old man was so disappointed that all the Bibles were gone, he begged for one of the boxes that had contained a Bible.

Many Christians sped to Russia to spread the good news of the gospel, and many hungry hearts received it. I went with a church choir and had an opportunity to tell a Bible story to young Russian children who had never heard of Noah. Their teachers said, "Tell us more." Now other politically correct liberals try to treat God like a nobody, but prayer became the order of the day on September 11, 2001.

What hope is there for this world and all the people in it? Without God, no hope at all! Without God we are all nobodies. No wonder people feel that life has no meaning.

When you don't know where to go or what to do, look

up. Even if the sun is not shining now, it will shine again. Look around you. Today people can find help on the World Network of Prayer sponsored by the United Pentecostal Church. *Guideposts* magazine lists a prayer line. The Upper Room Ministries in Nashville has a prayer line. The church on the corner probably has someone who will pray with you. When I taught kindergarten, I asked the children to pray for me and their prayers were answered. May seeds of hope rise in your heart as you turn to Him to find hope.

Be careful who you ask for help, though. I remember we were trying to cut through back country roads to get to Corinth, Mississippi. We stopped and asked an older couple on the road for directions. "Torinth?" the man looked puzzled. Finally he said, "You can't get to Torinth from here!" We needed a better guide. Look for praying people filled with the Holy Ghost, people who have a pipeline to the mighty God in Christ Jesus!

Where do we go to find hope? Go to the Bible to find hope in the Lord. Even children need to hear about this hope from their earliest days.

CHAPTER 6

Children Need Hope

"God is an optimist. Every new baby born into such a world as this is proof that God still has hope for us," said Bodie and Brock Thoene in *Stones in Jerusalem.*

Years ago medical science erred with premature infants, keeping them in an incubator without their mother's touch. The babies only felt the gloved hand of a nurse or doctor. A child needs loving hands to impart love and security from the first day of his or her life.

Until abortion became widespread, the womb was the safest, most secure place in the world. Born with a cry into a cold world, the baby is quickly placed on the mother's breast. Close to his mother's heartbeat, the baby finds food, comfort, and hope. But abortionists view unborn babies as fetuses with no rights.

Even third-world parents provide more hope for little ones. In a flimsy tree house a few feet above swirling floodwaters, Sophia Pedro gave birth to a daughter, Rositha. A helicopter later rescued Pedro, her disabled husband, the newborn daughter, and two other children. Sophia and her family escaped with nothing except her husband's precious crutches that he had waited so long to receive. He had lost a leg in the civil war in Mozambique, but his family was now safe from the flood. In the desperate situation in the flooded land, this story provides a bright spot of hope for families. In the midst of death, there can be new life, new hope!

If a strong mother and father continue to hold on to hope despite trouble and trials, their child learns to trust. He communicates with smiles and baby talk. He staggers to his feet and begins to explore the world and participate. He helps put his toys away and other small tasks. Encouragement and loving discipline guide him. His parents are his security. They build trust, hope, and love. Their children respond with love and trust.

A famous singer was booked for a performance in a popular opera house. A sold-out house, all the town talked about the coming event. Well-dressed cream of society eager to hear the acclaimed soloist packed the house. At the last minute, the performer fell very sick. Quickly the manager arranged for a substitute, then stepped on the stage to make the announcement.

"Boos" rang so loudly that the name of the new singer was scarcely heard. The stand-in singer sang her heart out, giving it her very best. When her final song was sung, silence reigned. No applause. Then from high in the balcony a little girl stood up and shouted, "Mommy, you were wonderful!" Immediately the crowd responded with a thunderous ovation. The Bible tells us that "a little child shall lead them." (See Isaiah 11:6.)

Unfortunately in today's world, a child may find it difficult to trust everyone. In September 13, 2002, *The Tennessean* newspaper, a boy and his sister were taken from their mother's home and placed with a family friend. When the mother was unable to speak to the girl for several days, she went over and was horrified to find her daughter's body in the friend's garage. When questioned the friend said he got angry thinking the girl was "using" him, then he strangled her. What a tragic story of misplaced hope and trust!

A letter from an orphanage told about two little girls, six and seven, who had been exposed to shootings and dangerous situations. One had been molested by her father, who was later jailed. They stayed briefly with any relative who would take them. Finally an aunt took the responsibility of caring for them. Then her health deteriorated, so she contacted the Children's Mansion. Hopefully there the girls will learn to trust God and find hope.

Mission newsletters carry stories of abuse and suffering of children worldwide. The *Friends of Sudan* carried a story by Edward Barnes first published in *Life* magazine, June 1992.

Hunted by lions and hyenas, living on leaves and bark, swarms of boys wandered the wilderness in a nation ravaged by a long and bloody civil war. Abandoned by adults, they fought a heroic battle for survival in their Republic of Children.

Since the mid-1980s, Sudan, located in East Africa, has experienced brutal civil war. Fleeing the violence and bloodshed of Sudan's internal conflict, thousands of innocent children have experienced mind-numbing horrors and internal hardship. Orphaned children as young as five years old carried baby brothers and sisters as they fled for their lives—not knowing where they were going or what the future held.

Trekking hundreds of miles on foot through the hostile East African desert, many children died of starvation, thirst, or attack by wild animals. Survivors told how they watched vultures feed on the bodies of their dead friends. They ate leaves to stay alive. Miraculously thousands survived that ordeal, finding refuge in camps in Ethiopia and Kenya. There the children—mostly boys—formed their own "family" groups. Older children protected the younger ones. Relief workers named the children the "Lost Boys." They clung together to escape a hostile adult world and find hope.

In his book, *Rebel with a Cause*, Billy Graham's son, Franklin, told about an experience in Rwanda, a war-torn African country. A million and a half people had died during the conflict between the Hutus and the Tutsis. Graham managed to get doctors, nurses, and supplies in to help the Rwandan people. As the Tutsis were fleeing Kigali, they would come upon small children sitting beside the decaying corpses of their parents. They roamed the hills "like packs of wild animals" with no one to care for them. That first day in Byumba, Graham saw a peculiar sight. A little girl sat alone in the back of a pickup truck. As she clutched a torn, bloodstained blanket, she rocked back and forth, eyes glazed, quietly singing.

"Who is she?" Graham asked a nearby soldier.

"Who knows?" the soldier replied.

"Is she singing in French? What is she singing?" Graham wanted to know.

The soldier leaned close to the child, then said, "Jesus . . . loves . . . her . . . " He paused. "No . . . me . . . something like that."

Then Graham asked, "Did she sing, 'Jesus loves me, this I know for the Bible tells me so'?"

"Yeah, that's it!" the soldier replied.

Then Graham said, "All she has left is what faith in Jesus her parents must have taught her!" The plight of the orphan so touched Franklin Graham that he raised funds and established an orphanage for 350 in that country to give children hope.[1]

Neglect, abuse, and harmful hurts at a young age instill doubt, fear, and loss of hope. This may make it difficult for the children to trust in a loving God. They need a friend to give them hope.

When my sister's oldest grandson, Jonathan, was only ten, he had trouble breathing. They took him to his pediatrician, but the doctor could not find the problem. Back home Jonathan still could hardly breathe. Back to the doctor they hurried. He gave no help.

Later in desperation, they rushed Jonathan to Vanderbilt Hospital. My sister called friends and relatives for prayer. Finally one doctor diagnosed his trouble as mediastinal lymphoma, a condition associated with non-Hodgkin's Lymphoma. Jonathan had to undergo a procedure that would cut through the muscle in his neck in order to biopsy the mass (said to be big as a grapefruit) growing in his upper chest.

The mass in Jonathan's upper chest was placing pressure on the superior vena cava, causing his trachea to narrow and his breathing to become more difficult. The surgeon located the tumor mass just in front of the internal jugular vein. While he was attempting to free the mass from being imbedded, Jonathan turned blue and could not be adequately ventilated. The surgical team stopped and tended to the immediate need of repositioning Jonathan and restoring adequate airway. The biopsy was then completed without incidence of cardiac arrest or further difficulties.

We all rejoiced and thanked God for their finding the right diagnosis and correcting the problem. Jonathan is now grown and the father of my sister's first two great-grandchildren. Prayers and hope in a dark night spared a little boy who could hardly breathe.

October 26, 2002, is a night Janice Jentzsch will never forget. Raised in a Pentecostal home, Janice is a professional musician. My mother gave Janice her first piano lessons. Here is her story:

"Our adopted son, Dalton, was visiting his biological father across town. I looked at the clock and thought, 'It's about time for Dalton to come home.'

"When Johnny, Dalton's father, called us in a few minutes, he screamed, 'Dalton has been burned and is on his way to the hospital!' Shocked, I could not speak. All I could do was pray and cry. Then I said, 'We'll meet you at the hospital.' Horror left me speechless, but Johnny said that Dalton would be okay. 'It's just his legs and his hand.'

"When we got to our local hospital, they told us that Dalton had been sent to Vanderbilt Burn Center in Nashville. I knew then that whatever had happened was catastrophic, and I began to silently beg God to spare my boy's life.

"I called Mom and Dad (Bill and Ruby Hughes) to meet Dalton at the hospital since they lived closer. Thirty miles passed in slow motion. Terribly shaky and nervous, yet outwardly I stayed calm and focused. The peace of Jesus shielded me from the storm that was coming. The moment of truth came when I walked into Dalton's room. Being burned is a tragically painful way to be injured. At that time, I was more concerned with his pain and disfigurement. Later I found out that Dalton would be critical for weeks and that his chances of dying of infection were high.

"When I got to the children's emergency room at Vanderbilt, a little girl was throwing up in the lobby. Crying babies added to the total chaos. Admitting clerks seemed to be walking and typing in slow motion. In the hall beyond, I saw my mother. 'Thank God, Mom and Dad are here!'

"Soon they admitted us to Dalton's room. A little bleary-eyed from the morphine, he sat up and tried to drink chocolate milk. He had told my dad that he loved him and that he had almost had a heart attack. He looked like he wanted to cry when I came to the bed. Big blisters totally covered his right hand. It seemed to me that had I tried to hold his hand that his skin would have slipped right off. He had some type of pressure covering on his stomach and legs. 'He is severely burned there,' they said. His left foot was blistered also. But the only mark on his face was a quarter-sized raw area. His hair had been singed as well as his eyelashes and eyebrows. I shuddered, realizing how close that fire came to him! All the hair on his arms had been singed off, yet there was no injury to his face, chest, or arms.

"Apparently he had tried to light a tiki lamp, and the

fuel can exploded in his hand. His clothing caught fire. Quickly Johnny had rolled him in a blanket. This quick action probably helped him to survive the fire.

"'He's critical and will be in intensive care,' the doctor said. Then they took him upstairs to clean the wounds, cut away the dead skin, and apply bandages. When we saw him again, he was dressed from his shoulders to his toes in layer after layer of bandages. Wires and tubes came out everywhere. Mercifully they gave him medication so that he could sleep. All I could do was pray, 'God, help him to heal fast and help him with the pain.'

"The pain came! Day after day the dressing changes became nightmare sessions that left me weeping as I listened to him pleading, 'Stop! It hurts!' I cried all the way to the hospital, all the way home and continually asked God 'Why?'

"Dalton would look at me with such pain in his eyes and ask, 'If Jesus loved me, why did He let this happen to me? Didn't He love me?' I did not have an answer. Every day I would pray with him and for him. Sometimes he asked me to sing a Jesus song to him.

"When the nurses came to move him or change the bandages, he would grip my hand and ask, 'Pray, Mom, pray!' It was hard for me. I felt that my faith had gone with the wind! Yet I had to be strong for Dalton.

"When he had skin graft surgery, all the skin on his back was peeled off and put onto his legs. Dalton was truly in terrible pain as the graft site left exposed nerves. He lay for four days on his back as the special dressing continued to leak his bodily fluids around the staples that held it to his back. I'll never forget the smell of those dressings!

"One day as I came in the room, the nurses had managed to get him to sit in a chair so they could change his bed. The first time he walked, he screamed the whole time that we were torturing him, but he did walk. Although it was like watching him take his first steps all over again, we began to have a little hope.

"Finally after two intensive weeks, all the tubes and wires were gone. He spent three weeks at Stalworth Rehabilitation Hospital, where he learned to walk, put on his clothes and grow stronger. He started in a wheelchair, then graduated to a walker. Finally he came strutting down the hall on his own two feet! When he got in trouble with the nurses because he was having a rowdy wheelchair race with his cousin, Justin, I knew he would be okay. Although Dalton's legs were terribly scarred, he was the healthiest kid on the whole ward. Most all the kids there were brain injured from car wrecks or had inoperable tumors. Many of them would never walk again or have a chance at a normal life. How could I say my pain was the worst when I looked into the eyes of the father of a fifteen-year-old girl who had been in a wreck and would never walk again? Or what could I say to a mother whose thirteen-year-old son would never talk or walk again due to a brain hemorrhage? The sound of Dalton's laughter and noisy procession down the hallways assured me that we were blessed.

"Dalton's legs are still very scarred today. They are red and purple with thick, puffy skin. He has to exercise every day to make sure that his legs don't start to draw up and cripple him. He has to wear a pressure garment twenty-three out of twenty-four hours. The pressure garment is like a tight long underwear made of girdle material. Hot and very hard to fit into. He missed two months of school but has done a wonderful job of catching up. He no longer has nightmares about fire. He is able to talk a little about the accident now, which shows that he is healing emotionally. He goes swimming three times a week. The doctors tell us that in a few years we will scarcely be able to tell where he was even burned.

"Many friends and family prayed for us, brought food to us, gave us gifts for Dalton, money to help with expenses, sat at the hospital for us when we could not be there, and lifted our spirits when we were low. The God that I had blamed for not loving me was showering His love on us every day throughout this horrible experience.

"I told Dalton that the devil had wanted to end his life, but God saved him and brought him out of the fire. Whenever Dalton looks in the mirror at himself, he sometimes says, 'My poor legs, my poor little legs.' I tell him that his scars are marks of courage, a reminder that he was a very brave boy who had survived with God's help and love. He seemed to accept that well enough, but I would think about it and wonder just how it all fit into my life. Despite the good outcome, I still asked God, 'Why?'

"Easter season rolled around. Time to consider the death of our Lord and Savior. I tried to imagine the pain our Savior suffered that we could be saved. I thought about the wounds of Jesus, with His scourged and bleeding back, His pierced hands and feet, the wound in His side. Then it hit me. When I kissed the little red spot on his head where Dalton had been burned, Jesus reminded me that He once bore wounds on His brow. When I rubbed lotion on Dalton's scarred back that had once been laid open and raw, Jesus reminded me that He had suffered the stripes on His back for our healing. When I looked at his scars on his stomach, which went from his side all the way across, Jesus reminded me that His side had been pierced. When I held his hand with the puffy skin grafts, Jesus reminded me that His hands were pierced. When I put Dalton's scarred foot into the pressure garment each day, Jesus reminded me that He had once had nails driven through His feet. Everything that Dalton suffered, Jesus had already been there. God revealed to me that He was perfectly aware of the human condition. (Even Jesus felt forsaken as He hung on the cross. He asked, 'Why?') Rather than feeling forsaken by God, I now know that He loves me and gives me hope that He is able to carry me through the worst storms of life.

"Dalton's interests in matters of faith have also grown. He is beginning to ask all sorts of questions, including the big ones like, 'Who made God?' and 'Can God hear you thinking?'"

I remember the saying, "An unexamined life is not worth living." Perhaps it's true of our faith. "An unexamined faith isn't worth believing in." From doubt to faith, from despair to hope, from grief to joy, God is always there ordering our steps. He does not sleep nor slumber, and He never makes a mistake!

Janice and Dalton's trial by fire left them with renewed faith and hope. But what about those children whose parents were not Christian, who were not disciplined, loving parents? I think of Bill Wilkerson, who is the pastor of one of the world's largest Sunday schools in New York. When he was a child, his mother left him on a busy corner of a large town in Florida, saying she would be back. He waited and waited but no one returned. Finally after three days, a Sunday school teacher of a Pentecostal church picked him up and took him home with him. After he grew up, he found the Lord and wanted to become like that loving teacher. So he chose the poorest section of this country's largest city, New York, and began to minister to the children there. He buses children into church, then through the week conducts sidewalk Sunday schools from the back of a truck to minister to thousands of lost and neglected children.

The Apostolic Pentecostal Church at 13th and Gravois, located in the heart of St. Louis, has ministered to hundreds of children for many years. I remember the Saturday night services where small children were encouraged to participate and sang solos, gaining hope and confidence while "Learning to Lean" on Jesus.

Hebrews 4:16 says, "Let us therefore come boldly unto the throne of grace, that we may obtain mercy, and find grace to help in time of need." Children need hope.

Deuteronomy 6:7 says, "And thou shalt teach them diligently unto thy children, and shalt talk of them when thou sittest in thine house, and when thou walkest by the way, and when thou liest down, and when thou risest up." That's a lot of teaching!

In a letter from The Children's Mansion, April Shaffer told of a young girl who had just met her father. She was excited. Sadly the father never returned. The girl wept bitter tears, holding tightly to the few possessions she had from him. The lack of a father's love will doubtlessly color that girl's image of a heavenly Father. The British poet, George Herbert, penned, "One father is worth more than a hundred schoolmasters."

So no matter how hard it is for us mothers and fathers to work and provide for and protect our children, we must "fit our backs to the burden," pick up our responsibilities and rejoice, knowing that "children are an heritage of the LORD" (Psalm 127:3).

A church paper recorded the story of Domine Keprotich, five years old, who went astray while following his brother into a forest in Kenya in 1995. Weeks went by, but the family could not find the little boy. Three years later, his father was killed by an elephant. In the spring of 1999, the mother was converted. She shared the story of her lost boy with her new friends. The pastor called for a special prayer meeting for the missing boy. After twenty-one days of fasting and prayer in May 1999, a report came from a neighboring village regarding an unidentified child. Three days later, the mother came marching home with her lost boy. A lost child found hope!

Before Christmas 1987, hope helped a kindergarten-age boy in a Philippine ferry disaster. About four thousand persons lost their lives in the world's worst peacetime sea tragedy—worse than the sinking of the Titanic. The little boy clung to a piece of wood for hours. The day after the tragedy, a fisherman sighted the child and rescued him. In trouble, a little child grabbed an unsinkable part of the wreckage and clung to it. He refused to give in to despair but kept on hoping for help. A little child held on to hope!

In a *Good Housekeeping* article, Wayne Kalyn called hope a powerful, proactive mind-set to instill optimism in kids. "Hopeful kids are positive about the future because they have overcome problems and succeeded in the past. So they believe they can do it again," says C. R. Snyder, Ph.D., professor of clinical psychology of the University of Kansas. "As one success builds on another, hope takes root and flourishes."

Sow Seeds of Hope

Parents can sow seeds of hope in their children. "Parents can really change the way children think about themselves and the world," says Lela Elliott, a family counselor in Buford, Georgia. "They can plant the seeds." How? To a large extent, by example. "Parents can actively transmit hope to their sons and daughters by how they themselves view the future, and how they cope, plan, and solve problems," says Timothy Elliott, Ph.D., an associate professor at the University of Alabama at Birmingham.

Robert Brooks, Ph.D., a clinical psychologist at Harvard Medical School, said, "I'm fond of saying to parents that if they can give any gifts to their kid—even more so than intelligence—it should be hope."

The article further said, "Don't wallow in weakness but spend time in strengths. If your child is weak in math but strong in art, help one and encourage the other. Kids need to feel that they contribute to their world and that they are respected and needed. If that's not hope, nothing is."

A Christian doesn't need an educator to remind him to "Train up a child in the way he should go" (Proverbs 22:6). Faith-filled parents know that God answers prayer, and they cling to hope.

Every child deserves a loving, caring mother and a protective, strong father to guide him and teach him to trust and hope when he goes into a wider unknown environment of kindergarten.

For over thirty years, we owned and operated West Nashville Kindergarten and Nursery school, starting with just a few children in the basement of our home in 1954. At that time, I had four children of my own including a two-year-old and a three-year-old. We began in September with only one child. By spring we had twelve. In 1962 we built a new school designed to care for seventy-five children with a staff of four teachers and a cook.

The whole idea started with a class my husband took on child psychology. "Why don't we turn this basement into an early childhood center. You can take care of other children while you care for ours." So a need spurred an idea, a hope of a better life. It succeeded far beyond our dreams—to more than a hundred children.

Daily surrounded by so many children, I noticed some who were trusting, happy children, ready to play, eager to learn. But a beautiful curly-haired blonde seemed okay until nap time, when she pulled out her hair. Each day I gathered up a handful of hair around her cot. One day her dad came roaring up on a big motorcycle for his visit with her. As he sped off, I was angry because of the risk of a small child on such a vehicle without even a helmet. Her mother told me, "If we had tried half as hard to save the marriage as we have tried to keep the divorce from hurting her, we could have saved our home."

Divorce destroys children's hopes and dreams. In the book, *Second Chance*, by Judith Wallerstein, she shares astonishing research. In a fifteen-year study following the lives of children of divorce, she found that they were still hurting. She asked Steve—a thirty-one-year-old mail-order clerk—if he ever thought about his parents' divorce, which happened when he was six. His response was swift and unforgettable: "No way. If I thought about it, I'd probably think a lot about it. I probably wouldn't be able to think about anything else. So I don't."

The broken families found it particularly hard to handle the holidays. Wallerstein conducted this study among middle-class families, mostly college educated parents, but few of their children went on to college. Their hopes were destroyed early. Few were able to marry and establish happy homes.

Wallerstein extended her study to twenty-five years. She was astounded to find that the children of divorce still suffered from what she called a "divorce culture" even into their adult thirties.[2]

A dear friend was a child of divorce. Her father left home at Christmas, and she said for many years she could not enjoy Christmas. "Even today when my brother and I (both in our forties) get together, we talk about what our life would have been like had our parents not divorced."

Wallerstein said the women in divorce had a lawyer, the men had their lawyer, but no one really addressed the needs of the children. Perhaps churches could consider programs not only for men's ministry and women's leadership classes but also counseling for the hurting children of divorce.

Boys raised with single mothers often feel a lack of a strong male role model. Dr. James Dobson has a bestselling book, *Bringing Up Boys*, which deals with that problem.

I was shocked when I researched the suicide problem to discover that suicide was the third leading cause of death among children. How essential it is to hold on to hope! Loss of hope not only destroys us, it also destroys our children. But if in our hurts we turn to God, we can say with Jeremiah, "It is of the LORD's mercies that we are not consumed, because his compassions fail not. They are new every morning: great is thy faithfulness" (Lamentations 3:22-23). Indeed His mercies carry us from failure to bright hope.

CHAPTER 7

From Failure to Hope

"*We . . . rejoice in hope* of the glory of God. And not only so, but we glory in tribulations also: knowing that tribulation worketh patience; and patience, experience; and experience, hope: and hope maketh not ashamed; because the love of God is shed abroad in our hearts by the Holy Ghost which is given unto us" (Romans 5:2-5).

Glory in tribulations? In a talk at a church, Lisa Beamer, widow of Todd Beamer who was killed in the 9/11 attacks, talked about walking humbly before the Lord, accepting what comes our way. "He hath shewed thee, O man, what is good; and what doth the LORD require of thee, but to do justly, and to love mercy, and to walk humbly with thy God?" (Micah 6:8). She said further that we must accept what happens to us each day—even on September 11, as the will of God concerning us.

Ludwig van Beethoven's (1771-1827) life seemed hopeless. His mother, pregnant with her fifth child, had tuberculosis. Her drinking husband had syphilis. Their first child was born blind, the second died. The third was born deaf. Should she have aborted the fifth? We can be glad she didn't, for if she had, there would have been no Beethoven. He became deaf after 1818. He had to converse by writing, but he wrote great symphonies after he was deaf. He still had music in his soul.[1] He had hope despite his loss of hearing.

The dreams and hopes of children sometimes do encounter disappointment and discouragement. When the Schuller farm was blown away in a tornado, Robert Schuller's parents were no longer able to pay for his college. He worked two jobs, which meant he had very little time to study. His English grades dropped to an F and his professor told him to forget writing. "You'll never be a writer." Robert Schuller never gave up hope. He has written many bestselling books.

On the other hand, some people are born with great opportunities. Luke 15:11-32 tells of a young man who had it all. His father was a prosperous man and a generous loving father, but tales of faraway places enticed the young man. The lovely homeplace bored him. "Nothing ever happens around here," he probably thought. Brazenly he went to his father and asked for his share of the estate. Then off he hurried to a riotous life. Lots of friends, feasting, life in the fast lane. But a famine arose, the economy failed, fair-weather friends disappeared. The prodigal son woke up broken, friendless, homeless, almost hopeless.

"I'll get a job," he thought, but jobs were scarce. Finally he found one job, but his employer said to this Jewish boy, "You can feed my pigs." "I'll take it," he quickly agreed. Hungry he chewed on the husks he fed to the hogs. Then the Scripture tells us that he came to himself. "What am I doing here? Dad's hired hands have food. I'm going home and try to get a job at Dad's." He knew where his best hope lay.

Many people fail from time to time, but they are never defeated as long as they keep getting up again. Thomas Edison failed repeatedly trying to make the incandescent light bulb. His usual reaction was, "Well, now we know another way that *won't* work." Even when a fire destroyed his main research center, Edison said, "All our *mistakes* burnt up."

In World War II, the British seemed defeated at Dunkirk. But they quickly gathered all the ships in England, however small, and rescued their soldiers from the German army. Hitler thought he was winning, but Winston Churchill made his stunning speech: "We'll fight them on the beaches. We'll fight them in the streets. We'll never, never, never give up!"

Roosevelt listened to that speech. He decided that despite some isolationists in Congress, he would find a way to help our "cousins." So he developed the Lend Lease law. Hitler also listened to that memorable speech. He wondered, "Do the British have a special secret weapon?" He decided to divert his army to Russia. The terrible Russian winter and the long supply lines weakened Germany and helped defeat her. One man with a "never give up" attitude turned despair into hope and tragedy into triumph.

Samuel Johnson said, "It's worth a thousand pounds a year to have the habit of looking on the bright side of things." Someone has said, "If you look at the ground, you may find a dime, but if you look at the sky, you may get a million-dollar idea."

Thomas Carlyle dared to dream again. While he wrote the first volume of the history of the French Revolution, he suffered almost total poverty and defeat. He felt that this was his greatest work and would surely bring him literary success. When he finally finished that first volume, he took it to John Stuart Mill to read.

Mill sat by the fire and carefully read the manuscript page by page. The next morning the maid gathered up the pages which she thought he had discarded and built a fire with them.

When Carlyle heard about this, he felt defeated and depressed. Then one morning he looked out a window and saw a man building a wall one brick at a time. As he watched he decided to start over, one page at a time.[2] Carlyle went from failure to hope.

Wilma Rudolph wanted to be an athlete, but polio crippled her. With the encouragement of her mother, she set out to overcome her handicap, walking daily, gradually building up strength to run. At last she ran in the Olympics, winning over tremendous odds. Rudolph went from failure and pain to hope and victory!

The dreaded polio struck Jackie and J. D. Stephens when they were children. Jackie recovered with no ill effects, but J. D. was left severely crippled. He does not let that hinder him. He has a family, a successful business, and is active in his church. Now in his fifties, he has a new kind of brace. For the first time, he was able to wear tennis shoes. I asked J. D. one day, "Do you always hurt?" "Not at all," he said cheerfully as he went limping on his way. J. D. went from failure to hope.

After my back problems, I began to notice how many people dragged one leg, how many used crutches or a walking stick. Over eighty percent of people past sixty-five suffer from arthritis. A beautiful young girl that I know lost her entire leg to cancer. She goes flying by on her crutches wearing an elegant high-heeled shoe on her remaining foot. Sunday's newspaper carried a story about a ballet dancer who lost a leg to cancer. He invented a new dance using his remaining leg and his elbow. He said, "Gotta keep dancin'."

We show what we are by what we do with what we have. So the wise person focuses on what he can do. Self-pity is such a waste. One school uses this motto, "A mind is a terrible thing to waste." Read the Bible to keep your mind stayed on hope. Its precepts, principles, promises, and persons will guide us. The Bible gives many examples of people who went from failure to hope in Him!

The Tennessean printed an article about Jerry Dahmen. He has interviewed hundreds of people who have overcome impossible odds and shared their stories on WSM Radio program, "I Love Life." He has identified five ingredients that brought hope and happiness to people. He called this "The P.O.W.E.R. Plan." It consists of Purpose, Overcoming the "BUTS" with commitment, Watching out for the "I can't" syndrome, Expressing fears, and Reaching out with faith.

Dahmen asked twenty random shoppers in a mall

what their mission in life was. Only two responded with a specific answer. The others didn't have a clue. A middle-aged man said, "I'm too old to think about that stuff—never get what I want I anyway." Another said, "I'd just like to sleep until noon the rest of my life and forget about anyone else." These people need hope in Him.

Our youngest son, Joe, had difficulty deciding on a career. One blazing hot summer, he helped his brother, Jeff, insulate low-income houses in East Tennessee. Joe decided he definitely did not want to do that all his life, so he enrolled in college. His father said, "Take a business course. You will always have to manage your own business." Joe finished at the University of Missouri, St. Louis, and is now in charge of the computer work in a large company, feeling challenged and successful in his choice.

The July 27, 2001, issue of *The Tennessean* featured the story of James McCune, a houseparent at Tennessee Children's Home, a home for children who have had a minor brush with the law or a disrupted family. McCune challenged these youngsters in a unique way. Behind his house in Springfield on one and a half acres, he shows them how to garden. Kids from the city who didn't know an onion from a weed now know about picking peppers, squash, tomatoes, and other good things that turn a weed patch into delicious dinners. The boys have found out that it's a lot of trouble tilling, sowing, weeding, watering, then finally reaping. "It's a lot of hard work," said one boy wiping sweat from his face. "I'm learning how to make money honestly," added another.

The teens staff a roadside farm stand Tuesdays and Thursdays after 6.00 P.M. and all day Saturday. Traffic slows to a trickle as people stop to buy "the best corn in the county!" "Last weekend was our best yet," one boy said. "We made six hundred dollars!"

What a great way to teach about life, sowing and reaping. This teaches lessons that hold hope for tomorrow. The boys learn to till the soil, digging out rocks and weeds, sow the seed, then wait for the harvest of their labor. They learn to work like it all depends on them, then they discover that a lot depends on God's weather.

McCune says that the garden is like a metaphor. "These boys have had weeds come up in their lives and choke them, so we try to cultivate the boys and help them grow. They see how important it is to pull up the weeds of doubt, despair, discontent and sow patience, love, grace and mercy that they may enjoy 'the fruit of the Spirit . . . love, joy, peace, longsuffering, gentleness, goodness, faith, meekness, [and] temperance' (Galatians 5:22-23)."

A child raised in a small-thinking family, school, or community may tend to become a person of limited vision. My husband grew up on a sharecropper's farm. Later his father got a job in a cotton mill village. The Bemis Bag Company furnished good housing, a company store, a good school, a community church, a YMCA, a place for gardens, hogs and milk cows. The company furnished everything to keep the working families happy.

At age fourteen, my husband started working in the mill. School hours were set so that the students could go to work at 2:00 P.M. After graduating from high school, many of them stayed on at the mill and worked for the company until retirement. But J. O. Wallace wanted more education. That was in the thirties, during Mussolini and Hitler's day. Even J. O.'s parents discouraged him. They said, "The Lord is coming soon."

J. O. wanted to go to engineering school at University of Tennessee. He could work for tuition, but he had no money for books and living expenses. He went to Lambuth College in Jackson, Tennessee, for a while but continued working a full night shift at the mill. Soon his eyes began to fail him, so he dropped out. Then he went to Memphis to Draughn's Business College and studied accounting. Shortly after finishing that college, he drew a low draft number. "I'll soon be drafted so I'm going home for a while." He met his father, J. W. Wallace, when he got off the bus. "Where are you going?" he asked. "I'm going to Nashville to start a church. Come, go with me," J. W. Wallace invited his son. So J. O. went with his father to help found the first Pentecostal church of our faith east of the Tennessee River.

Within the year, J. O. was in the army. When he was discharged, he resumed college, attending Bob Jones College and later George Peabody College for Teachers, now a part of Vanderbilt University. He left the mill company behind and prepared to work for God.

David wrote many of the Psalms during dark, difficult, desperate days. Paul wrote most of the Epistles while in prisons. John Bunyan wrote *Pilgrim's Progress* from a jail. While too sick to move from her bed, Florence Nightingale reorganized the hospitals of England. During much of his life, American historian Francis Parkman suffered so acutely that he could not work for more than five minutes at a time. His eyesight was so wretched that he could scrawl only a few gigantic words on a manuscript, yet he contrived to write twenty magnificent volumes.

In 1873 Horatio Gates Spafford, his wife and four young daughters planned a wonderful trip to Europe. As their departure drew near, his business required Spafford to stay home. He kissed his family good-bye, promising to join them soon. Off the coast of Newfoundland, their French steamer, the SS *Ville du Harve* collided with an English sailing vessel and plunged to the bottom of the frigid sea in twenty minutes. Anna Spafford prayed with her girls, holding the youngest in her arms. As the icy water swept the decks, the three older girls disappeared. Even the baby was washed from her mother's arms. Finally Anna was picked up by a lifeboat.

Ten days later the survivors landed in Wales and Anna wired her husband, "Saved alone!" Immediately Horatio sailed to England and was reunited with his grieving wife. D. L. Moody, a close friend, joined the bereaved couple. They affirmed their faith saying, "It is well. The will of God be done."

Later Spafford wrote the beautiful poem, "It Is Well with My Soul." Paul P. Bliss set it to music. It is now a universally applicable hymn bringing hope and courage to many when they face tragedy.[3] The Spaffords found peace and hope despite the wreck at sea.

Pain can be a prison or a prism. Paul in a dank, dark prison suffering with his thorn in the flesh reflected the light of God's glory in his great letters of encouragement. "There was given to me a thorn in the flesh, the messenger of Satan to buffet me, lest I should be exalted above measure. For this thing I besought the Lord thrice, that it might depart from me. And he said unto me, My grace is sufficient for thee: for my strength is made perfect in weakness. Most gladly therefore will I rather glory in my infirmities, that the power of Christ may rest upon me. Therefore I take pleasure in infirmities, in reproaches, in necessities, in persecutions, in distresses for Christ's sake: for when I am weak, then am I strong" (II Corinthians 12:7-10). Paul's words ring the bells of hope two thousand years later!

Paul Tournier says that perhaps the most powerful and unused gift from God is choice. Dan Dean wrote a great song about choices, "I Choose to Be a Christian." We can choose hope and bring triumph out of tragedy just as Paul did. Paul Claudel said, "Jesus did not come to explain away suffering or remove it. He came to fill it with His presence."

Tim Hansel told about reading a story that Mary Moore had written about her terrible third-degree burns suffered in a scalding shower. A burn unit in a hospital is a terrible traumatic place when burns have to be debrided and skin grafts begun. In the midst of all that pain, she met a man known simply as Sarge. Although his burns were far worse than hers, he continually offered her and others a cup of coffee, a glass of juice. He brought hope and life and love to a traumatic place.

One evening as they talked, he told her that in just a few more operations he would be able to go back to his wonderful wife and children. His wife had just graduated from college. Mary inquired, "What college?" When he told her, she was stunned.

"Sarge, that's a black college. Your wife isn't black, is she?"

He was quiet for a long moment and then said, "Yes, ma'am. What color did you think I was?" Her tragic accident had given her the privilege of meeting a man who would teach her how to see the world through different eyes.[4] Race was almost obliterated behind the burns and scars.

From Failure to Hope

On September 11, 2001, survivors, rescuers, firemen, policemen, businessmen, and women alike were covered with ash. Black, red, yellow, and white men and women were just humans, all alike. Race or gender was not a factor.

The army officer who gave the order for the napalm bombing in Vietnam was told that the village had been vacated. He checked twice but was assured that everyone was gone. When the bombs were dropped, however, one family had been left behind. One of the soldiers took the picture of the naked nine-year-old girl burning with arms outstretched running for her life. That awful picture was shown around the world. When the officer saw it, he realized that he was responsible for that horror. He never spoke of it but carried a terrible load of guilt. The little girl survived, and the Communists sent her to Cuba to spread propaganda against the U.S. Later she took refuge in Canada. She spoke at the Vietnam Memorial Day ceremony and said she wanted to offer forgiveness for the tragedy. Meanwhile the officer had gone to college and become a pastor. He was there that day and they finally met. The young woman assured the pastor of her forgiveness. As Samson said in Judges 14:14, "Out of the strong came forth sweetness." It takes a strong woman to forgive such a terrible tragedy.

On a radio call-in show featuring Barbara Johnson, a caller reeled off an incredible barrage of pain and frustration including an alcoholic husband, a gay son, and an unmarried daughter who was pregnant. The woman asked for help. Dumbfounded Barbara could think of no advice. Finally she blurted out, "God only knows!" The crowd began to titter, and the talk-show host chuckled, then

Barbara remembered a favorite scripture in Deuteronomy 29:29: "The secret things belong unto the LORD our God."[5] Only God can bring hope in such horrible situations.

CHAPTER 8

Seniors Need Hope

One wit said, "After you're forty, it's all maintenance!" As seniors sometimes we think we are at the end of our rope. Health problems, financial problems, pink slip on the job, midlife crisis, marriage problems, problems with children, both the young and the old. What does the future hold? Is there any hope for seniors?

Herbert Lockyer, a minister, did not begin writing until after he retired. He wrote numerous books such as: *All the Men of the Bible, All the Women of the Bible,* and *All the Occupations of the Bible.* My favorite is his book *Dark Threads the Weaver Uses.* Here Lockyer tells the story of his wife's battle with Alzheimer's disease. He took

107

care of her until her death in her nineties, then wrote this beautiful tribute to marriage. In a hopeless situation, he did not yield to despair but brought hope to many who may suffer a similar situation.

Recently a friend stopped in the bookstore to buy a tape of Sunday's message. "It's for my brother-in-law," she said. "He's a Baptist minister. This was his first visit in our church. He's a good man. For many years, his wife has suffered from a disease that has left her helpless. He resigned his pastorate, bought a Greyhound bus and remodeled it into a mobile home. They travel constantly. He parks their bus and preaches revivals. His wife requires almost complete care, but he 'keeps on keeping on.'" Let's pray that the sermon on the meaning of Pentecost Sunday will help him understand that he can have Holy Ghost anointing on his life!

Later Pat Tuggle told me about meeting a senior at her doctor's office. The eighty-year-old woman had been in a terrible car wreck in the seventies. Her husband was killed, and she was hospitalized for weeks. While she was incapacitated, someone broke into her house and stole her valuable antiques. Later she moved to Tennessee to be near her son. She built a duplex saying, "Someone may need to move in with me." Her father did move in, and she cared for him until his death. Later another relative needed to move in with her. She told Pat that when she got through at the doctor's office, she was going home to paint her back deck. Pat was astonished at the attitude of this eighty-year-old. This senior wasn't just waiting to die. She cared for others, stayed busy, and lived in hope.

Nancy Reagan said, "A woman is like a tea bag, You

don't know how strong she is until she's in hot water." Mrs. Reagan proved to be strong in her love and care of President Ronald Reagan as he struggled with Alzheimer's.

A sixty-three-year-old woman from Nashville wanted to climb the highest mountain in Africa. Despite a bad knee, she took a knee bandage and lots of ibuprofen and left to climb that mountain. The view from the top was worth it all to this determined woman.

Beth Stein, a reporter for *The Tennessean*, wrote about her mother-in-law's move to a retirement community. She noted that the seniors seemed to have a sense of dignity that is sometimes missing among younger people. The ladies wore colorful summer dresses and were well-groomed. The men wore jackets and demonstrated kindness by pulling out chairs and other gracious courtesies. Although some shuffled on walkers and dragged oxygen tanks, most seemed to be in fairly good health. The atmosphere radiated congeniality. Then it occurred to her that she was observing an era whose days may be numbered. "The gentility that is a way of life for that generation may be quickly passing. In most restaurants and even in many churches, casual is in, dress-up is on its way out. We will all be the poorer for it," Stein said.

When depression and loss of hope sets in, personal grooming often goes begging. "I just can't find the strength to even comb my hair today." Job 11:15-18 says, "For then shalt thou lift up thy face without spot; yea, thou shalt be stedfast, and shalt not fear: because thou shalt forget thy misery, and remember it as waters that pass away: and thine age shall be clearer than the noonday; thou shalt shine forth, thou shalt be as the morning." Great hope for seniors!

In the seventies, we visited a most remarkable missionary in Thailand, Elly Hansen. A native of Denmark, Elly survived World War II, helped Jews escape from the Holocaust, trained as a nurse, then went to Thailand as a missionary. She worked in a leper colony, founded an orphanage, and established a mission in Thailand. After hearing about the Holy Ghost, she sought that blessing. When she received the Holy Spirit, her mission board refused to continue to support her, but she stayed on. Elly's Thailand friends took care of her.

Later our Pentecostal church began to support her. When she came to the U.S. to solicit funds, she stayed a few days with me because I wanted to write her story. After ten hours of taped interviews, I put the project aside due to other pressing deadlines. Elly returned to Thailand. Months later I heard that she had cancer. We flew to Thailand to get the final information for her story, and I completed her biography before she died. What a remarkable woman! From being the daughter of a bartender, she became a dedicated senior missionary who never lost hope.

Doris Haddock, ninety years old, stepped out first from Pasadena, California. She finished her thirty-two-hundred-mile walk fourteen months later standing on the U.S. Capitol steps. She had walked ten miles a day, fourteen hundred steps to the mile into our hearts and history for the cause of political campaign finance reform. She was hospitalized for dehydration in the Mojave Desert, saw the bluebonnets bloom in spring in Texas and trudged through the snow in Pennsylvania, but Doris kept walking.

Life is a journey through deserts, over mountains, down valleys, through heat and cold, good times and bad times. Haddock, widow and a great-grandmother, raises a standard of purpose and persistence especially to all seniors. No moping, whining, sitting in a nursing home. She found a purpose and pursued it. She had hope.

Listen to this quote, "This is the beginning of a new day. I can waste it or use it for good. What I do today is important because I am exchanging a day of my life for it. When tomorrow comes, this day will be gone forever—leaving in its place something I have traded for it. I want this to be gain, not loss; good, not evil; success, not failure, so that I may not regret the price that I paid for it" (Anonymous). God gives all of us 1,440 gifts. Every one has the same. Time, not riches, is our greatest asset. So make every minute of the 1,440 minutes of your day count for Him.

Someone has said, "Maturity is understanding that you don't need to understand." Just keep singing, "We'll understand it better by and by," a song of hope that seniors have sung for years.

In 2002 J. O. and I celebrated our sixtieth wedding anniversary. Neither of us really expected to live that long. J. O.'s parents died before they could celebrate their fiftieth anniversary, so we celebrated with a special party on our fortieth. Ten years later on our Golden Wedding Anniversary, our children honored us with another celebration such as my folks had enjoyed. For our sixtieth, we took our children to Charleston, South Carolina, to spend a special week together. But J. O. wanted a party also, so we entertained over a hundred family and friends in our home.

When young people asked, "How do you stay married sixty years?" I answered, "One word, *whatever*!" That word has settled many a tense moment. Hope kicks in and happiness follows.

Helen Hallums plans the senior activities in our church. What a great example and role model she is. She began attending Sunday school in the West Nashville Pentecostal church as a young girl. She worked at a grocery store and attended George Peabody College for Teachers. She worked her way through college earning a master's degree in special education. Married with four children and a handicapped husband, she not only taught special education classes in the metro school district but continued to work in the grocery store. Her children grew up and two of the girls married and have children. Helen cared for her mother the last five years of her life and also a brother for four years. Her son, Freddie, still lives at home. A highly intelligent, responsible, gifted woman, she plans for the seniors with delightful trips and other activities. Her life has had its share of pain and problems, but Helen has met them with courage, commitment, and hope.

"Pain is part of being alive, and we need to learn that. Pain does not last forever, nor is it necessarily unbearable, and we need to be taught that," said Harold Kushner, who wrote the book, *When Bad Things Happen to Good People.*

I have found that to accept and embrace the pain makes the pain bearable. When I am busy doing something, writing this book, managing the church bookstore, or even listening to a friend sharing her problem, I forget that numb left leg and its pain.

Henri Nouwen explains, "Each human being suffers pain in a way no other human suffers. Pain is personal and comparing pain brings no comfort or consolation.

We human beings can suffer immense deprivation with great steadfastness, but when we sense that we no longer have anything to offer to anyone, we quickly lose our grip on life. Instinctively we know that the joy of life comes from the ways in which we live together and the pain of life comes from the many ways in which we fail to do that well."

Isn't it amazing that despite the news that over 100,000 people die every year of hospital errors, we often wait until the last minute to call for the "elders of the church" as James instructed us in James 5:14? "Why are some people so resilient? How do they deal so well with setbacks?" Preachers and philosophers have always relished such questions. Now, after a century of near silence, scientists are asking them, too. Words like *optimism* and *contentment* are appearing with ever greater frequency in mainstream research journals—and some enthusiasts foresee a whole new age in research psychology. As University of Pennsylvania psychologist Martin E. P. Seligman declares in his new book, *Authentic Happiness*, "The time has arrived for a science that seeks to understand positive emotion, build strength and virtue, and provide guideposts for finding what Aristotle called the 'good life.'" In a study of identical twins, Auke Tellegen surveyed 732 pairs and found them closely matched for adult happiness, regardless of whether they'd grown up together or apart. Such findings suggest that while we all experience ups and downs, our moods revolve around emotional baselines or "set points" we're born with.

A second lesson is that our circumstances in life have precious little to do with the satisfaction we experience. Paul said in Philippians 4:11, "I have learned, in whatsoever state (circumstance) I am, therewith to be content" (parentheses added). Married churchgoers tend to outscore single nonbelievers in happiness surveys, but health, wealth, good looks, and status have astonishingly little effect on what the researchers call "subjective well-being." Even paraplegics and lottery winners typically return to their baselines once they've had six months to adjust to their sudden change of misfortune or fortune. People living in extreme poverty are, on average, less happy than those whose basic needs are met. But once we cross that threshold, greater wealth stops making life richer. People in Japan have nearly nine times the purchasing power of their neighbors in China, yet they score lower in surveys of life satisfaction. In America, notes Hope College psychologist David Myers, real income has doubled since 1960. We're twice as likely to own cars, air conditioners, and clothes dryers, twice as likely to eat out on any given night. Yet our divorce rate has doubled, teen suicide has tripled, and depression has increased tenfold. Somehow, we're not cut out for the ease that comes with wealth.

Seligman talks about our obsessive concern with how we feel. Is our life productive or meaningful? He terms "gratification" as the enduring fulfillment that comes from developing one's strengths and putting them to positive use. Gavagan and Beamer faced a horrible tragedy at 9/11 and decided to use what they had to help someone else despite the fact that both widows have three children each to rear.

Shortcuts to happiness often turn out to be detours. Sandra Murray, a psychologist at the State University of New York at Buffalo, has found that the best married couples are not the most realistic but the most positive. They idealize their partners and expect their relationships to survive hard times. The larger the romantic illusion, the better the odds. People who idealize their mates may be quicker to forgive small transgressions. And people who are idolized may try harder to please their partners. Do you see the glass half-full or half-empty?[1]

Brother Lowell H. Benson, former district presbyter of the Tennessee District of the United Pentecostal Church, grew up as an orphan, living with his grandparents. He came to St. Louis as a teenager. There he got acquainted with Brother Odell Cagle, found the Lord, received the Holy Ghost, and felt a call to preach the gospel. He and Brother Cagle held a revival for our small country church in Finley, Tennessee. He married the most beautiful girl there, Nina King, and began a busy successful life as a minister. Then he was stricken with tuberculosis which left him with weak lungs. Now eighty-eight, he still preaches. When he gets in the pulpit and begins to preach, his voice rings loud and strong.

Seniors often suffer pain. After his terrible accident while mountain climbing, Tim Hansel, author of *You Gotta Keep Dancin'*, finally met a doctor who said there was nothing he could do for him medically. "I suggest that you bite the bullet (of pain) and live to 100." "Does that mean the ball is in my court? From here on out it's up to me?" "Absolutely, the choice is yours."[2] Hansel chose to write a book on hope to help us all.

I faced a similar situation in 1995 and found Hansel's book most inspiring. Ever since I fell down the stairs, I have suffered severe back pain. I broke my leg. They fixed my leg, but they did not X-ray my back. After a rear-end collision outside Birmingham, I went to have my back X-rayed and the doctor asked, "When did you break your back?"

"I didn't know it was broken."

"Here's an old break," he said.

I went from one doctor to another for several months. They all said, "There's nothing we can do." Spinal stenosis was their final diagnosis. Finally I went to the best neurologist in Nashville. He looked at all the tests and X-rays. Then he asked, "Mrs. Wallace, are you sure you want to have back surgery at your age? I cannot make you like new. Maybe relieve a little of the pain."

"I can handle the pain," I answered. So after therapy, I learned how to walk using a quad cane. I just try to embrace the pain. It is a numb sort of tingling constant feeling—not unbearable so I try to ignore it. I rarely ever take pain pills. Too many side effects. I had read Norman Cousins' book and knew attitude meant much. Cousins said, "Scientific research has established the existence of endorphins in the human brain—a substance very much like morphine in its molecular structure and effects. It is the body's own anesthesia and a relaxant and helps human beings to sustain pain."[3]

God has been good. I can walk around the house with my quad cane. Hansel's book is a tremendous inspiration, so I keep hobbling along—not dancing—but at least moving with the help of my wonderful husband. Pain and suffering help us realize who we are in Christ Jesus. Listen to David in Psalm 139:1-14:

"O LORD, thou hast searched me, and known me. Thou knowest my downsitting and mine uprising, thou understandest my thought afar off. . . . If I ascend up into heaven, thou art there: if I make my bed in hell, behold, thou art there. If I take the wings of the morning, and dwell in the uttermost parts of the sea; even there shall thy hand lead me, and thy right hand shall hold me. . . . For thou hast possessed my reins: thou hast covered me in my mother's womb. I will praise thee; for I am fearfully and wonderfully made: marvellous are thy works; and that my soul knoweth right well."

So I will do what I can, then trust God for the rest! One writer said it well, "I'd rather attempt to do something great and fail than attempt to do nothing and succeed."

Elizabeth Elliot, widow of Jim Elliot, martyred by the Auca Indians, told us that Jim said, "He is no fool who gives all for what you cannot keep to gain what you cannot lose." Elizabeth returned to the field and served as a missionary to the Aucas. Later she married again, but that husband died also. Her writing style is completely different from Barbara Johnson's, but the courage to rise above adversity is similar.

Seniors who have lived through floods and tornadoes know that stuff can be replaced. It's life that is precious. When my daughter, Rosemary, worked as head nurse in charge of a nursing home in Corinth, Mississippi, she introduced me to several of the patients. They gave glowing remarks about "Miss Rosie." There with all the old folks was a young male paraplegic who wanted so badly to go to college. I hope he made it. Life gets very basic for a paraplegic!

An older man said, "As I get older, I seem to place less importance on material things." Then he added, "Come to think of it, I place less importance on importance."

I used to place importance on getting new clothes for

the general conference of my church. But after shopping hard one day, I suffered the next day with my hip. When I went to the doctor who sent me for an MRI, it showed a small fracture. Oh, no!

The doctor said, "I think it will heal itself if you will absolutely stay off it for two weeks." I did as he said, then went to a walker for two weeks. Finally he said, "You can go to your conference but use the wheelchair." My husband kindly pushed my chair. I told my friends, "I brought my Cadillac and my chauffeur!"

Seniors often have long prayer lists. At our General Conference in Phoenix, I talked with Margie McFarland, whose husband had died that summer. When I complimented her beautiful pink dress, she said, "I bought a black dress before Robert died, but he told me to take it back. 'Wear a pretty pink dress for me!'" Death was not a black horror for Robert McFarland, but a beautiful pink sunrise.

In his book, *You Gotta Keep Dancin'*, Hansel told the story of a young man who was desperately seeking God. "He sought out a wise old man who lived in a nearby beach house and posed the question: 'Old man, how can I see God?' The old man who obviously knew God at a depth few experience, pondered the question for a very long time. At last he responded quietly: 'Young man, I am not sure that I can help you—for you see, I have a very different problem. I cannot *not* see Him.'"[4]

Hebrews tells of those "who have fled for refuge to lay hold upon the hope set before us: which hope we have as an anchor of the soul, both sure and stedfast" (Hebrews 6:18-19). One writer described three kinds of anchors: the lunch anchor which was small and used just briefly in very calm waters, the working anchor, fitted to the size of the boat and used under normal circumstances, then the storm anchor which was heavier and stronger and kept for emergencies in very turbulent waters. Hope is our storm anchor. We can anchor our lives on God's plan and purpose and His promise to be with us throughout all the storms of life.

On vacation we enjoyed relaxing at St. George Island, Florida. The ocean seemed to go on forever. J. O. started some soup to simmering on the stove, then napped on the couch after a long walk on the beach. St. George was peaceful with no newspaper headlines screaming about Iraq. Palm trees and sea oats blowing in the wind. Shrimp boats in the distance drifting at anchor. Restful to drift at anchor and rest in His promises.

Later J. O. talked with the older couple who were walking the beach with their small dog. Suddenly a big owl swooped down and tried to snatch the puppy. Isn't that like life? Everything seems peaceful and calm, then a monster tries to snatch our peace and hope. The song says, "Some through the fire, some through the flood, some through the water but all through the blood." Life is sacred, special, and stupendous when we have hope.

Last summer the storms were firestorms out west. Many acres of forest burned as well as some homes. A speaker told about fire flowers. I love flowers and have always been interested in them, but I had never heard of this kind of flower. Called a fire flower, it only blooms after forest fires. Certain pines only grow after a forest fire. The cone lies there until a fire releases the seeds. The storms of life, whether fire or flood, either destroy us or reveal us. There are only two ways to approach life—as a victim or as a gallant fighter. A great theologian once said,

119

"There is only one miracle. It is life! We cannot waste the miracle of life on the trivial."

There can be the blessed hope even in death. When Maggie Carson, ninety-two, lay dying for eighteen days, her children, grandchildren and friends sang hymns, read Scripture, and prayed by her bedside. Lena Russell, eighty-six, who suffered an aneurysm, lay for three days until all her children, grandchildren, and one favorite brother had arrived. She wanted the chance to say good-bye. Seniors with hope in Him.

Hope means the most when we face the stark reality of death as did Dietrich Bonhoeffer. Bonhoeffer died for his faith, but even dying people die more peacefully when they have hope, either for recovery or for heaven. Bonhoeffer had a choice to collaborate with the Nazis or stand for his faith. Choice, not chance, determines destiny. One writer said, "Death is God's way of saying, your table is ready." What a blessed hope!

Two questions that bother us when we are in pain and have problems: Why and How? Why has this happened to me, Lord? How can I cope with this problem? Dr. Larry Crabb, a Christian psychologist and author of *Inside Out*, asked a pertinent question in a seminar. "Do you use God to solve your problems? Or do you use your problems to find God? All too often we are looking for a quick solution or some way we can fix the problem when we should be learning something about the 'theology of suffering.'" One counselor commented that "those who suffer well and keep a passion for God in the midst of their pain are often called saints."

Never forget that God is in charge. He said in Jeremiah 29:11 (NAS), "I know the plans that I have for you . . . a future and a hope." One writer said it well, "The iron crown of suffering precedes the golden crown of glory."

Robert Fulghum in one of his bestselling books talks about the "Uh-Oh frame of mind." Try to see life's catastrophes as momentary difficulties rather than horrendous tragedies. "When you see something as 'Uh-Oh,' you don't have to dial 9-1-1."

Barbara Johnson suggests that we write down our problems, each burden in a separate envelope. Then in prayer lift each envelope to God. Tell it to Jesus alone as the song says. Tell Him all about it. Let this be the last time you will speak of it. Then whisper, "Take it, Lord. Only you can handle it."[5]

Just for today, Lord, I'll turn my burden over to You. I can do something for one day that would stagger me if I felt I had to discipline myself that strictly for a lifetime. Happiness is indeed a choice so I'll turn my burdens over to You, put on a bright red sweater, get out of the house for a while, and catch a glimpse of hope!

sow seeds of hope

CHAPTER 9

Catch a Glimpse of Hope

"The righteous hath hope in his death" (Proverbs 14:32b).

Peggy Jenkins wrote the following testimony of Jerra K. Gadd.

"George drew me aside in the hospital linen closet to tell me what was going on. It did not look good. In an emergency room crib lay our second daughter, Garnna, just thirteen months old. In a coma, she was hooked up to life support, IVs, and all kinds of tubes and equipment. What a terribly frightening scene!

"'We need to practice what we believe,' George

whispered as he held me close. 'God's ways are not always our ways.'

"That time and place changed our lives forever. We began to live by I Thessalonians 5:18: 'In every thing give thanks: for this is the will of God in Christ Jesus concerning you.' Although we were just twenty and eighteen years old, we gained a spiritual maturity beyond our years as we stood in the closet and determined to live out that verse.

"That righteous act of thanking God—even through Garnna's death from spinal meningitis that night in 1961—offered us an unbelievably sustaining hope in the years ahead.

"It sustained us in 1972 when our twenty-seven-month-old daughter, Shelam, died of a brain tumor. Though it was not made easier in those ten years and five months, we clung to the hope God promised through His instruction to 'Thank Him in all things.' The hope that if we obeyed, we were still in His will, still under His care.

"What a loss we suffered with the next death to strike, that of our twenty-nine-year-old daughter, Carrie, a young mother of two-minus-one, having lost a son in childbirth. George and I encouraged each other with the precious hope-verse we had long ago memorized: 'In every thing give thanks: for this is the will of God in Christ Jesus concerning you.' Our other children— Daniel, Joseph, Lamech, and Sharek—heard us quote it often, observed us living it resolutely.

"When Carrie died from flu complications in 1989, we had been struggling with Danny and Joe's health problems for many years. Both of them suffered from brain tumors similar to Shelam's. In 1991 when Danny succumbed to death at age twenty-nine, we engaged the faithful promise God had given us—our hope lay in obeying and *trusting God*. Once again we thanked God for His many blessings, for Danny's life of love and service, and his death in the Lord. Oh, how that sustained us!

"We relinquished Joe into God's hands in 1992, also at age twenty-nine. George determined to write of these experiences in a book and title it, *No Stranger to Death*. Before that could come about, however, George died on December 16, 1996.

"I clung to our verse—alone. It was enough. God sustained me through even the death of my loving lifelong mate and continues to help me each day. God is my source of peace, joy, and life, so I will give Him thanks in everything, *'for this is the will of God in Christ Jesus concerning you* (and me!).'"[1]

Our amazing Lord drops just the right inspired scripture when we need it most. This is true if we hide His Word in our hearts.

In his book, *A Future and a Hope*, Lloyd Ogilvie tells of an old Scots couple whom he visited in Scotland. The old friend was eager to show Ogilvie his collection of antique pieces of armor, especially the collection of helmets. As he examined the metal of one helmet, his friend explained, "The helmet was one of the most important parts of a suit of armor. It protected the warrior's head and his brain. Under surprise attack, it was important to get the helmet on, or you might not get the rest on." Over the shelf on which Andrew had arranged the helmets . . . he had placed a placard which read: "Mind Yer Head an' Serv' the King!" Hang out with happy, hopeful people. Avoid the negative doomsayers. Put on the helmet of hope.[2]

Once we have caught a glimpse of Christ Himself as our hope, the next step is to allow Him to control our thinking. Proverbs 23:7 says, "For as he thinketh in his heart, so is he."

In Luke 24, the two on the road to Emmaus met "Hope" but failed to recognize Him. Sometimes we place hope in the wrong places. Samuel placed his hope in Saul. He failed to realize that Saul's disobedience caused God to reject him.

This next illustration tells how a little boy finally caught a glimpse of hope:

"On a cold dark night in a blizzard in Chicago, a little newsboy asked a policeman, 'Do you know a warm place where I could sleep tonight? I've been sleeping in a box around the corner.' The policeman said, 'Go down to that white house. Knock on the door and say, John 3:16.'

"Although he had no idea what John 3:16 meant, the little boy knocked on the door and said to the kind lady who answered, 'John 3:16, ma'am.' The lady seated him in a splint back rocker in front of a roaring fire in a fireplace. As he rocked and warmed himself, he said, 'I don't understand John 3:16, but it sure keeps a cold boy warm.'

"After a while, the lady asked, 'Are you hungry?'

"'Well, I haven't eaten anything in two days,' the boy answered. She set him down to a table loaded with good things to eat. After he had eaten his fill, he thought, 'I don't understand John 3:16, but it sure fills up a hungry boy.'

"'Do you want a bath?' the lady asked.

"The boy answered, 'I had a bath a long time ago

when they flushed out a fire hydrant.' Then the lady took the little boy upstairs to a shining white bathroom, took off all his dirty rags, and helped him into a tub full of warm water. As he scrubbed his dirty neck and ears, he said, 'I don't understand John 3:16, but it sure cleans up a dirty boy.'

"After dressing him in warm pajamas, the kind lady took him into a bedroom and tucked him into a soft feather bed. As he drifted off to sleep, he murmured, 'I don't understand John 3:16, but it sure gives a tired boy some rest.'

"The next morning the kind lady read the Bible in front of a roaring fire as the little boy rocked in the rocking chair. She told him about Jesus and the plan of salvation. 'Now do you understand John 3:16?' she asked.

"'I'm not sure I understand all about John 3:16, but it sure makes life worth living!' the boy declared as he caught a glimpse of hope.

"Well said!"

(Author unknown)

Jesus said, "If you are ashamed of me, I'll be ashamed of you before my Father in heaven." Scripture after scripture assures us that life on this earth is not all there is to know. These scriptures will help you catch a glimpse of hope:

"The righteous hath hope in his death" (Proverbs 14:32).

"To day shalt thou be with me in paradise" (Luke 23:43).

"I am the resurrection, and the life: he that believeth in me, though he were dead, yet shall he live" (John 11:25).

"For we know that if our earthly house of this tabernacle were dissolved, we have a building of God, an house not made with hands, eternal in the heavens" (II Corinthians 5:1).

"If in this life only we have hope in Christ, we are of all men most miserable" (I Corinthians 15:19).

"And God shall wipe away all tears from their eyes; and there shall be no more death" (Revelation 21:4).

Hope beyond the grave helped Negro slaves to sing about angels and heaven.

I looked over Jordan, and what did I see,
Coming for to carry me home?
A band of angels a-comin' after me,
Coming for to carry me home.

Blind from birth, Fanny Crosby wrote hundreds of beautiful songs. She sang of her hope of eternal life.

But oh, the joy when I shall wake
Within the palace of the King!
And I shall see Him face to face.

In the midst of the Great Depression, we sang songs similar to, "When I Take My Vacation in Heaven" and "The Mansion over the Hilltop." During those terrible financial difficulties in the thirties, we caught a glimpse of hope and sang about mansions. John Hagee said that losers talk about what they are going through; winners talk about where they are going to—that mansion over the hilltop.

The hope of life beyond this life inspires man to live

nobly and sacrificially today. My friend, Fred Kinzie, wrote so well about how we gain *Strength Through Struggle* in his book by that title.

Many a woman goes about her simple duties in the midst of despair and hopelessness. To run from problems only compounds them. Usually there are meals to prepare, dishes to wash, floors to mop to give some semblance of normalcy, a glimpse of hope.

The devil tries to destroy the hope of all mankind, but the old rugged cross on Golgotha symbolizes hope for all the world. Crosses now stand high on steeples of beautiful Christian churches. On 9/11 at the tragedy of the World Trade Centers, workers were amazed to find crosses in the midst of the debris. Life is full of hills and valleys, despair and doubt, but we know who made the hills and the valleys. Look closely and you can catch a glimpse of hope in the deepest valley.

My friend, Regina Ormond, lost her only daughter, Shaina, in a terrible three-wheeler accident. Another friend, Helen Stallones, lost her daughter in sickness. My sister, Jane Young, lost her little girl, Carol, at age eleven to leukemia. My ninety-year-old cousin, Gladnie Hilficker, lost her daughter, Barbara, to cancer. These women form a sisterhood of suffering. They know, "It's a terrible thing to bury your child." It's out of order. Parents should die before children. How can they catch a glimpse of hope?

Only the hope of life beyond this vale of suffering makes that kind of trial bearable. I cannot say, "I know how you feel." I can only hug them and point them to the hope beyond the grave. In our valleys or on our hilltops, we can look for the cross and the door of hope and lift our voices in songs of worship, "On Christ, the solid Rock, I stand; All other ground is sinking sand."

Paul wrote in Romans 15:13, "Now the God of hope fill you with all *joy* and peace in believing, that you may abound in hope, through the power of the Holy Ghost" (italics added). My mother's Bible was heavily underlined in Paul's writings of the hope and the grace of God. This hope we have in God overflows joyfully as we surrender to the power of His Holy Spirit.

Some Christians don't seem to want to be happy and hopeful. As a result, they remain miserable, spreading gloom and despair. One writer said, "Some people divorce hope and marry despair." But God didn't save us to be miserable. Read John 15:16, "Ye have not chosen me, but I have chosen you, and ordained you, that ye should go and bring forth fruit, and that your fruit should remain: that whatsoever ye shall ask of the Father in my name, he may give it you." Forget the past. "Brethren, I count not myself to have apprehended: but this one thing I do, forgetting those things which are behind, and reaching forth unto those things which are before, I press toward the mark for the prize of the high calling of God in Christ Jesus" (Philippians 3:13-14).

I remember a dear friend of mine who lived in a small town. Her husband was repeatedly unfaithful to her. Years later I asked her if she would write her story anonymously for a book I was getting together. "Why, Mary Martha," she said, "I've almost forgotten that." She caught a glimpse of hope, saved her marriage, and the couple lived peaceably to a ripe old age.

God offers to make us fruit bearers. He is always ready for something exciting. Today is the first day of the rest of your life. Let us live on the edge of new developments, the cutting edge of life, hid with Christ in God. "Beloved, now are we the sons of God, and it doth not yet appear what we shall be: but we know that, when he shall appear, we shall be like him; for we shall see him as he is. And every man that hath this hope in him purifieth himself, even as he is pure" (I John 3:2-3).

A life without hope is like a car stuck in the mud, wheels a'spinning, going nowhere. But dig out the wheels, let friends, but especially the Word of God, give you a shove and drive yourself out of the muck and mire of hopelessness.

The apostle Paul talked about his changed life, his new lifestyle, to his fellow Christians in Philippi. "But what things were gain to me, those I counted loss for Christ. Yea doubtless, and I count all things but loss for the excellency of the knowledge of Christ Jesus my Lord: for whom I have suffered the loss of all things, and do count them but dung, that I may win Christ. . . . Not as though I had already attained, either were already perfect: but I follow after, if that I may apprehend that for which also I am apprehended of Christ Jesus" (Philippians 3:7-8, 12).

After the Damascus road experience, Paul had a completely new life. His goals, ambitions, and attitudes were totally changed. So he added: "Let us therefore, as many as be perfect, be thus minded: and if in any thing ye be otherwise minded, God shall reveal even this unto you. Nevertheless, whereto we have already attained, let us walk by the same rule, let us mind the same thing" (Philippians 3:15-16). When one catches a glimpse of hope in the Holy Spirit, it totally changes one's life, his ambitions, his goals, and his attitudes.

A glimpse of hope helps us to set goals—meaningful, measurable, and manageable goals. Success alone will never bring happiness. A meaningful life filled with passion for a purpose crowns a life. My father-in-law had such a purpose. He wanted to build Pentecostal churches east of the Tennessee River. He was past fifty when he started the first church. Sixty-nine years old on his deathbed, Papa insisted that he had one more sermon to preach. He never lost hope. He had meaningful, measurable goals, and he managed to achieve many of those goals.

My daughter, an RN, has a very responsible job in the corporate office of HCA, but last year she finished a bachelor's degree in information technology online at night. For relaxation she makes beautiful purses and paints pictures.

I tell all our children and grandchildren, "If you are at a standstill and hardly know what to do, go back to school or study something. Don't ever get mired down and waste time in front of a television. There's too much to do here in America. Possibilities range all around us. Catch a glimpse of hope and move on with your life."

In the business book, *Good to Great*, Jim Collins points out that the chief executive officers of great companies were not stellar executives like Lee Iacocca. But they were humble men who had a passion for their work. I remember when Brother N. A. Urshan, former General Superintendent of the United Pentecostal Church, asked my husband to manage the Pentecostal Publishing House. The company was in the red, and it was forecast that the next year would be even worse. J. O. thought the business could be turned around, so he began to work steadily. He asked me to serve as the editor.

That first year, we published fifteen books, which the churches bought gladly. I compiled one about pioneer Pentecostal women, and later wrote one about the pioneer pastor R. G. Cook. We had other manuscripts submitted which we published. We took displays to conferences. Pentecostals were hungry for their own books. We had found a need and began to fill it. J. O. turned the Publishing House around in one year and made a profit the second. We published about twenty books that second year. J. O. was drawing Social Security, so he only took the allowed amount as salary until he was seventy. By that time, the business was prospering nicely. He felt challenged by the work and stayed with it for twelve years. When J. O. retired, Brother Marvin Curry, his assistant, took over and the company continues to do well. A purpose, a goal adds meaning and hope to anyone's life.

Peter, a Galilean fisherman, left his nets and found his life's purpose in following Jesus. The thesis of his letter is suffering and glory. Fifteen times Peter referred to the suffering the saints in Babylon would soon face. But he encouraged them to hope to the end.[3] The iron crown of suffering will be replaced by the golden crown of glory. What hope!

Once we catch a glimpse of hope, find purpose for our lives, then we want to sow seeds of hope in the lives of our friends and loved ones.

CHAPTER 10

Sow Seeds of Hope

"Blessed be the God and Father of our Lord Jesus Christ, which according to his abundant mercy hath begotten us again unto a lively *hope* by the resurrection of Jesus Christ from the dead" (italics added) (I Peter 1:3).

Sam Moore, head of the world's largest Bible company, began his remarkable career as a door-to-door Bible salesman. A Lebanese by birth, he came to America, started selling Bibles and now is head of the famous Thomas Nelson Book and Bible company. Undoubtedly he did not timidly ask the women who answered his knock on their door, "You wouldn't want to buy a Bible, would you?" A confident, positive salesperson knows his product, is sold on it, and is eager to share his enthusiasm with others. Once we catch a glimpse of the mighty God in Christ who is our hope, we want to sow seeds of hope everywhere we go. We want to be God's salesmen.

Does your life seem like a tightrope between hope and despair, life and death? The Easter story symbolizes that struggle. The apostles, other believers, many women, Mary and her family knew of Christ's arrest, His beatings, then His slow painful death on the cross between two thieves. They stood afar off and watched the humiliation, the mockery, the hatred. They saw Joseph of Arimathaea lay His body in the sepulcher and roll a large stone in the door. The next day the Pharisees persuaded Pilate to seal the stone door and set a watch before it. All hope of the Messiah and a new kingdom seemed gone. They were a frightened, purposeless people whose world had crashed! They thought they had no hope.

Very early on the first day of the week, some simple women with a desire to do the right thing "came unto the sepulchre at the rising of the sun." This was another day. Certain chores needed to be taken care of. "But who shall roll us away the stone at the door?" they wondered as they carried the spices for their sad duty of anointing the dead Christ. The very act of coming and asking that question expressed some hope. Somehow they must have felt the stone would be rolled away. They had not totally surrendered to despair and gone to bed with a headache. Nothing indicates, however, that they expected the Resurrection. They just wanted to do what they could do.

People who have only a small grain of hope do not usually go to bed with a headache. They are not headshakers and hand-wringers. They get up with "the rising of the sun" and set out to do what they can do. Someone has well said, "When you don't know what to do, sow seeds." These women took spices to "sow seeds of hope" in a cold stone sepulcher.

The noun *hope* is not used in the Gospels. Only the verb *hope* is mentioned in Luke 23:8. Jesus did not need to talk about hope. He was and is our hope. "Christ is risen from the dead, and become the firstfruits (hope) of them that slept" (parentheses added) (I Corinthians 15:20).

I remember standing in the tomb of Christ (or what is supposed to be His tomb) in Jerusalem in 1977. Tears flowed and I trembled with emotion as I recalled the story of His resurrection.

Hope for all mankind was indeed born on Easter morn. Peter, Paul, and the New Testament writers used the word *hope* often.

Napoleon once acknowledged that he as a leader had inspired warriors to follow him to their death as had other great leaders such as Alexander the Great. Then he said that Jesus Christ was the only leader who could still inspire men to follow Him to their death hundreds of years after His own death. Two thousand years later, missionaries, preachers, and evangelists go everywhere—even to Muslim countries in the Mideast—sowing seeds of hope.

In his book, *Be Hopeful*, Warren Wiersbe writes about seeds that fall on shallow soil producing rootless plants. When our heart's soil has been broken and crushed, seeds of hope can produce tough faith. One writer said, "When the going gets tough, the tough get going." Trials come. They may be varied. They are not easy, but they are controlled by God. He said He would not put more on us than we could bear but with every temptation provide a way of escape. Wiersbe said further, "A faith that cannot be tested, cannot be trusted."[1]

We may fail miserably and hear a rooster's crow mock our lack of courage. Then, like Peter, we can turn to the resurrected Christ and learn to walk on water and feast at His table.

David in Psalm 1 talked about the man who walks not in the counsel of the ungodly, nor stands in the way of sinners, nor sits in the seat of the scornful (the cynic who thinks we Christians are hopeless!) "but his delight is in the law of the LORD. . . . he shall be like a tree planted by the rivers of water, that bringeth forth his fruit (more seeds for sowing hope) in his season; his leaf also shall not wither (green through all seasons of life); and whatsoever he doeth shall prosper" (parentheses added).

In that hard-to-understand, yet blessed story of Job, he tries to go forward, but God is not there, and backward, but "I cannot see Him. But He knows where I am, and when He has tried me, I shall come forth as pure gold." Old Satan tries to bring out our worst, but when we sow seeds of hope, Jesus can bring out our best.

In I Peter 1:6-7, the apostle wrote, "Ye are in heaviness through manifold temptations: that the trial of your faith, being much more precious than of gold that perisheth, though it be tried with fire, might be found unto praise and honour and glory at the appearing of Jesus Christ."

No goldsmith would deliberately waste that precious ore. He would put it into the smelting furnace long enough to remove the cheap impurities; then he would pour it out and make from it a beautiful article of value. An eastern goldsmith kept the metal in the furnace until he could see his face reflected in it. So our Lord keeps us in the furnace of suffering until we reflect the glory and beauty of Jesus Christ.

What can we do in the midst of fiery trials? We pray, we read the Word, we go to church, and we try to sow seeds of hope. We do the same things that we do when all is well. Like Quakers we try to center our minds and hearts on Jesus. Each trial teaches us something new about God. When Abraham became willing to offer his son as a sacrifice, he learned that God would not demand more than he could stand. Paul learned from his thorn in the flesh (II Corinthians 12) that not all prayers are answered. Some things have to be endured.

Joni Eareckson has spent most of her life in a wheelchair, paralyzed. Recently I read her latest memoir, *This Is My God*. In this book, she tells of her active childhood, riding horses, playing the piano, swimming. The youngest child, she tried hard to excel and usually did win out in most everything she tried. When she was about seventeen, she dived into shallow water. The accident left her paralyzed from the neck down. How can any of us complain of aches and pains when Joni writes books, paints pictures with the brush in her mouth, records CDs, and raises money for wheelchairs for disabled children in third-world countries!

Lloyd Ogilvie persevered when he was hurt. Christopher Reeves, totally paralyzed, raises money for research. One writer said, "Instead of getting hooked on drugs, try getting hooked on hope." Then you can go forth and sow seeds of hope successfully.

A young woman came into the bookstore recently to sell gifts for the store. As we talked, I told her about a prayer request that I needed an answer to. Then Sheila told me about her father, Vernon Haynes. A diabetic, he had suffered colon cancer and had to have his colon removed. Then he had kidney problems and had to go on dialysis. That day he was in the hospital having surgery for a valve problem with his heart. We had prayer right then. I have called her several times to see how her father was doing. Today he answered the phone with an upbeat voice assuring me that he was doing fine. He sowed seeds of hope in my heart with his cheerful, positive manner! Several weeks passed by, then Sheila called again to ask for prayer. Her mother had been diagnosed with cancer! Life keeps reminding us to keep on hoping, trusting in Him, our only answer.

It's important to keep a positive, faith-filled attitude and do what we can to help ourselves. When I fell and broke my left shoulder several years ago, my doctor advised therapy. Ten years earlier, I had broken my right shoulder, but my doctor did not suggest therapy. As a result, I can't raise my right arm even to my shoulder. When my doctor ordered therapy for the break on my left shoulder, I went to Vanderbilt Hospital twice a week for months. I regained ninety-eight percent use of my left shoulder. Patience, perseverance, and hope pay big dividends. Remember the kindergarten Sunday school song about: "Faith, hope, and charity; that's the way to live successfully."

I have prayed for deliverance from my back problem, but it has not happened. However, I am happy to say that the problem does not seem to be much worse than three years ago. I have learned to ignore the pain on most days and endure it on others. What cannot be cured must be endured. So when asked, "How are you?" I try to respond, "Doing well." It is well with my soul even if my back and my knee are hurting. The Jamaicans often respond to "How are you?" with "Not too bad!" We can always say that as well as sing: "On Christ, the solid Rock, I stand; all other ground is sinking sand."

Among my notes, I found this article from a senior newsletter taken from the *New Albany Informer*.

Learn to Live One Day at a Time

"We must learn to live one day at a time. If there is anything at all taught in the Sermon on the Mount, it is this lesson. Notice that Christ said, 'Take therefore no thought for the morrow: for the morrow shall take thought for the things of itself. Sufficient unto the day is the evil thereof' (Matthew 6:34)—that we must learn to live one day at a time. If you will notice unhappy people, miserable people, people that are troubled, even those who are mentally ill, they are people who have never learned this lesson. They live either in the past or in the future and try to mix them up with the present. They have not learned to live one day at a time. There is no difficulty, no circumstance, no problems which cannot be handled one day at a time—no habit that we might have which we cannot break, one day at a time.

"Christ taught this well in the Sermon on the Mount. Paul expressed it when he said that we must forget the things that are behind and press on daily to the things that are before. We cannot live in our future. We live always in the present. People who are happy and successful have learned to live one day at a time.

"Many of us live in the past. We regret things in the past. All of us have made mistakes. All of us have sinned. We must ask God to forgive us, and then we must forgive ourselves and forget these things. We have done foolish things in the past, but we can never correct all that is now gone by. Put it in the past. Sow seeds now for a future harvest of hope.

"Every day when you awaken, you have a new life that must be lived. Don't worry about what might happen in the future. Worry is paying interest on things that usually never happen, so let us count our blessings and name them one by one."

(Adapted)

So we put on the helmet of hope each morning and trust God for our daily bread and strength for the day. As we put on the armor of God, we purpose to sow seeds and take a stand for what we believe. We want to be a pipeline for the gospel, not a puddle of defeat and doubt. We all have our own set of problems. Over 100,000 Christians have been martyred for their faith. So we learn to give thanks in everything, for this is the will of God concerning us.

The people of *Guidepost* magazine sent me a small 2004 calendar that also included a poem by Mary Gardiner Brainard (1837-1905), which carries the same thought:

> I see not a step before me as I tread on another
> year;
> But I've left the Past in God's keeping—the
> Future His mercy shall clear;
> And what looks dark in the distance may
> brighten as I draw near.

CHAPTER 11

Reap the Harvest of Hope

In about A.D. *63,* Peter wrote in I Peter 1:3 about a lively hope by the resurrection of Jesus Christ. Warren Wiersbe wrote in his book, *Be Hopeful,* that it is glory all the way. Low lying clouds or prison dungeons may hide the face of the sun, yet we know that above the clouds the sun is shining. Sometimes in the drudgery of daily trials, despondency and despair set in, but hope in our Lord and Savior causes us to look up, for our redemption draweth nigh. We can reap the harvest of hope of heaven.

Peter knew that troubles and trials awaited the new Christians everywhere. Paul may have been in prison awaiting execution. Peter knew that he, too, was probably on the list.

Paul was martyred about A.D. 64. Perhaps that same year or shortly after, Peter was crucified. According to history, Peter requested to be crucified upside down. He did not feel worthy to be crucified as his Master had been. In the midst of all this persecution, Peter wrote about a lively *hope* that Christians reap through many kinds of trials, tribulations, and troubles.

Rome had not paid a lot of attention to the Christians when they thought they were just another Jewish sect. But their widespread growth caused Rome to take notice. The mad emperor, Nero, blamed the fire of Rome (July, A.D. 64) on the Christians. So serious trouble was ahead as Peter wrote this letter to encourage the new Christians. He wrote about suffering but also about glory. He encouraged us to "hope to the end" (I Peter 1:13), to not be ashamed of our hope but ready to explain it and defend it (I Peter 3:15). We know that we can never out-suffer our Lord Jesus Christ. Through seeds of suffering, we reap a harvest of hope in Him.

Just as our forefathers fought and died for America, so our Christian forefathers suffered and died for this precious truth. Read and reread Peter's letter until you feel that "lively hope" that will take you through "fiery trials" that the early church endured. You will reap a great harvest of hope!

Today Christians are still being persecuted and, in some Muslim countries, martyred. September 11, 2001, brought home to us in an earthshaking fashion, how much many Muslims hate Christians and Jews. They want to convert us or else kill us. The present war in Iraq demonstrates more about the deadly hatred that Muslims have toward Israel and America. However, hopefully, few of us will suffer the kinds of "fiery trials" that the earlier church endured.

In today's world, we do suffer from stress, depression, disease, and disaster. Peter's letter still encourages us to, "Use hospitality one to another without grudging. . . . minister . . . one to another" (I Peter 4:9-10). In the fellowship of other spirit-filled Christians, we can reap a harvest of hope.

Read Norman Cousins' books, *The Anatomy of an Illness* and *Head First: the Biology of Hope and the Healing Power of the Human Spirit.* Cousins tells us how often hope and a bright outlook cause a turn-around in a medical problem. Prayer changes things. Reach out for that lively hope. A Vanderbilt Hospital ad said, "The best weapon in the fight against disease is in your head." We know that our best weapon is our hope in Him!

Although faced with prison and martyrdom, Paul in Titus 2:13 wrote about looking for that "blessed hope, and the glorious appearing of the great God and our Saviour Jesus Christ." What a harvest!

Today we are not faced with the same trials that Peter and Paul experienced; however, Satan never gives up sowing weeds of discontent, discord, despondency, and despair in our lives. Discontent drives people to shopping malls to max out their credit cards for things that they really don't need. Things never fill that God-shaped place in our hearts. Only His Holy Spirit gives us godly contentment. Dave Ramsey, financial advisor and talk-show host, warns us that stuff will wreak havoc and lead to bankruptcy. Just one more thing is never enough.

Robert Schuller said it well, "Start small, think tall, invest your all and send out a call to heaven. No one is so poor that he has nothing to give."

Discord can cause a loss of hope. It's amazing how a hearing loss can impair relationships. One must learn to be patient with oneself as well as one's companion. "I'm sorry, dear. I didn't hear you." Don't give up hope. Remember the deaf girl who became Miss America.

Despair sets in as you try to pray with dear friends who face unbelievable trials. One of my dear friends faithfully visits her son who will remain in prison for twenty more years. She will probably not live long enough to see him freed. Why didn't he see that the lonesome road led straight to terrible trouble? Thank God for the bright hope she has in a beautiful granddaughter.

One late rainy afternoon recently, a middle-aged couple stopped by the bookstore. The woman went straight to the card rack and carefully hunted for just the right card. Her husband looked through the CDs of choir music, then restlessly prowled through books. I did not recognize them. When she paid for her cards, I asked, "Are you from out of town?"

"Yes, we just left our daughter at Mercy Ministry (a nearby home for troubled girls). We wanted to see where she would be going to church."

I reached for her hand and said, "We have a handicapped granddaughter who lives at a home for the handicapped. It's hard, I know." Tears flowed and I began to pray, "Lord, bless this daughter at Mercy Ministries. May she find peace for her soul and an answer for her problems." The mother wiped away her tears. Then she and her husband left on that dark, dismal rainy day for the long ride home to Texas. One more to add to my prayer list. Perhaps I had sowed a few seeds of hope.

Read I Peter 1:13. "Wherefore gird up the loins of your mind, be sober, and hope to the end for the grace that is to be brought unto you at the revelation of Jesus Christ." Christians live in the future tense. God's children always have. The Jews ate the Passover in haste, ready to move on out to the Promised Land. "And thus shall ye eat it; with your loins girded, your shoes on your feet, and your staff in your hand; and ye shall eat it (the Passover) in haste" (parentheses added) (Exodus 12:11).

In Hebrews 11, Abraham had his eye on the "heavenly city." Although he was promised the land, all he ever owned was the cave of Machpelah. There he buried Sarah. Later Isaac, Rebecca, Jacob, and Leah were buried there. But Abraham dug wells and gave hope to thirsty people and their cattle. When enemies plugged up the wells, instead of feeling hopeless, Isaac redug those same wells and drank from them.

Lot chose the well-watered plains, which appeared to be the best financial choice. He went to live in a wicked city, not realizing the awful price he would pay for momentary pleasure. Abraham brought blessings to his family. Lot brought judgment and disaster. Despite Lot's hopeless situation and terrible end, II Peter 2 calls him a righteous man. Read Lot's story. No one is hopeless.

Jesus met a Samaritan woman at Jacob's well in Sychar near to the parcel of ground that Jacob gave to his son Joseph. Jesus asked the woman for a drink. (See John 4:4-26.) She marveled that Jesus would even speak to her. Then He told her about water that if she drank it, she would never thirst again. To a hopeless, rejected woman who had been married five times and was now living in adultery, Jesus gave hope. God is no respecter of persons. He shows no partiality, and He accepts no bribes. The despised Samaritan woman and the haughty Pharisee, Saul of Tarsus, alike believed on Him and reaped a harvest of hope.

Remember we are only sojourners here. Do you recall that old song, "This World Is Not My Home"? When you are discouraged, focus on that heavenly home that awaits us, as you sing about the home beyond the blue.

Brother and Sister Norman Paslay, evangelists, sang, "We're a Happy People" as the theme song of their great evangelistic meetings. The Fred Kinzies sang a song about "You Cannot Wear a Smile and Wear a Frown." Singing songs sows seeds of hope.

David wrote in Psalm 46 about God, our refuge and strength. Verse 4 says, "There is a river, the streams whereof shall make glad the city of God." David had many ups and downs, hills and valleys, but God called him a man after His own heart.

Joseph, the favored son, a dreamer, stirred up jealousy in his brothers to the point that they threw him into a deep pit. Later they sold him into slavery. His dream became a nightmare. His father, Jacob, lost all hope when he saw that blood-stained robe of many colors.

Then Joseph found a prosperous place in Potiphar's house. But a trap in the guise of a wicked woman awaited him there. Joseph's character shines out. Genesis 39:8 states it simply, "But he refused." Here for better or for worse, Joseph's character was clearly displayed. He refused.

Potiphar's wife cried, "Abuse!" and, of course, her husband believed her. Again Joseph's future looked hopeless as he stared out prison bars. Pits and peaks! Dreams and despair! Is that a pattern and rhythm of life here in this world?

Genesis 39:21 says, "The LORD was with Joseph, and shewed him mercy, and gave him favour in the sight of the keeper of the prison." Staying busy helps one to have hope even in a prison.

Still not a bitter but a caring man, Joseph noticed two of his fellow prisoners sad and discouraged. As he served them, he asked, "Why are you so sad today?" They answered, "We have dreamed a dream, and there is no interpreter." "Don't interpretations belong to God?" Joseph said. Then he interpreted the dreams of his fellow prisoners, the baker and the butler. His interpretation proved to be correct.

When the butler was released from prison, he promised Joseph that he would remember him. But as fair-weather friends sometimes do, the butler completely forgot Joseph. Man may forget us, and God may seem silent, but the Lord never forgets His own.

For two more long years, Joseph served in that Egyptian prison. He kept on doing what he could do. Not whining, "Where are you, God?" Later Pharaoh had a disturbing dream which none of his wise men could interpret. Suddenly the butler remembered Joseph, the man who knew about dreams. Again Joseph went from the pit to the peak. Soon he served the king as his right-hand man.

Years of humiliation tested Joseph, but God brought hope for his entire extended family. In Genesis 45:7, Joseph saw the whole big picture, "God sent me before you to preserve you a posterity in the earth, and to save your lives by a great deliverance." Also Genesis 50:20 says, "But as for you, ye thought evil against me; but God meant it unto good, to bring to pass, as it is this day, to save much people alive." From dreams to nightmares, pits to peaks, humiliation to high places, Joseph's character is clearly displayed. It is always at moments like this that we see men most clearly. Joseph sowed plentifully in the good times, then reaped bountifully and spread hope for the Egyptians as well as his own family during the bad times.

An old Chinese proverb says: "In no prairie fires do the seeds perish. Watch the blades shoot forth among the spring breezes." All the flowers of summer owe everything to the seeds of spring. There's always something left. Burned to the ground? Perhaps, but the land was left. The ground never burns. Even tornadoes leave something.[1]

An architect friend of Dr. Schuller's was devastated when his dream home burnt. Dr. Schuller told him, "You have a lot left. The lot did not burn. You can rebuild." So the talented architect rebuilt an even finer home. Later he designed and built the Tower of Hope for Dr. Schuller's church in 1968. "My dream is to have America's first twenty-four-hour, crisis-intervention telephone ministry housed in that tower. Here we'll train hundreds of volunteers to answer the telephones and encourage persons who are in crisis—even suicidal." Since its opening, the lights have never gone out in the Tower of Hope.[2] Hurting people need to know that someone is praying.

Hope is like salt. It adds flavor and preserves. Hopeful people add excitement to a drab, dreary climate. We can bring fresh flavor and fragrance into a drab, dreary day. Hope restores the joy of living. Hope helps our dreams to come true.

Lord, let me flavor my surroundings and light my world with hope.

CHAPTER 12

Great Heroes of Hope

September 11, 2001, shook our hopes and destroyed our innocence to a great extent, but the raising of the flag at Ground Zero resurrected hope. A year later at a memorial service, Tim Chavez, writer for *The Tennessean,* wrote a stirring account headed, "Terrorists can bring buildings down, but they cannot destroy American spirit. And hope. The terrorists had intended to turn America into a crumbling fortress of fear." But Chavez insisted, "Instead they made it and us stronger."

In the foreword of the book, *Holding on to Hope,* by Nancy Guthrie, Anne Graham Lotz wrote about September 11. "Rescue efforts began as thousands of people systematically started combing through the debris to find survivors. One rescuer told how he had climbed down into a hole in the twisted steel and rubble and grabbed a hand. He extended his arm even farther to shine his flashlight. He reached back for someone to grab his hand. A human chain was formed and the man trapped in the pile of debris was pulled to safety."[1] These men were heroes of hope!

Gwen Shaw in her paper, *End-Time Handmaidens & Servants Magazine*, told of many who survived September 11. Mieko, a young Japanese woman married to a Korean/American, worked for a Japanese company on the eightieth floor of the Second Tower. That day she arrived at work early. By 7:30 A.M., she stood at a window looking at a beautiful sunny day. The Holy Spirit said, "Say the Lord's Prayer!" As she prayed, she felt that her life would never be the same. "Why?" she asked.

When the First Tower was hit, she heard a loud noise and saw fireballs. Her boss shouted, "This is an emergency! Tell everyone to leave right now." He hurried them out of the office, but he and the other supervisors stayed behind to search the washrooms. Mieko grabbed her handbag and, together with the rest of the staff, she started down the stairway. After twenty minutes, she got to the fifty-third floor, then she felt the impact of the second plane as it hit the tower where she was. The whole building shook. Everyone was filled with fear. "Pray!" she called to everyone.

On the way down, the Lord said, "Just keep praying. I have a reason for all this. Give me more of you." When she finally got outside, the firefighters shouted, "Go! Go! Don't look back!" But she looked, saw the dreadful sight:

people on the roof and hanging out the windows crying out for help. Most of her colleagues and her bosses were safe except the Japanese bosses and one college student who lost their lives trying to save others.

Bishop Joseph Williams, the Chaplain of the Year for the firefighters of NYC, was called to the scene immediately and told to wear his clerical collar. When he arrived, he saw bodies being loaded into refrigerated trucks. Many, many bodies. Eighteen members of his church worked either in the WTC or its vicinity. None lost their lives.

Suzette Gayle from Bishop Williams' church said, "My husband and I had an 8:30 appointment in the city, but I overslept. When I arrived on Chambers Street, the First Tower was already on fire. 'There's been an accident!' I thought. Then I saw bodies flying through the air to the ground. When I saw the second plane hit the South Tower, I knew it was an attack by terrorists. I started running for my life as the officers shouted, 'Run north and don't look back!'"

Jeanette Wilson from the church said, "I was working in the Finance Center. Five of us employees normally came early to pray, usually between 8:15 and 8:30. That morning I couldn't get out of my house. The train was slow, not moving. There were delays on the street. Finally they made us get off the train. When I asked why, they said, 'Catch the next train.' By the time I arrived, I was late. Every one of our group of five was late. Then I saw the fire. I cried, 'Oh, dear Lord! What will they do? How will the firemen get up that far to put the fire out?'

"I knew I could not go to work. I didn't know what to do. I couldn't move. While standing there, I saw the next plane hit the Second Tower. It blew up! Then I knew it was an act of terror. I didn't know which way to run. I didn't know where to go. I cried out, 'Help me, God! Keep the girls who are working in my office.' I didn't see a policeman anywhere. No one knew what to do. They were confused.

"All day I worried about my missing friends who I prayed with each morning. I was crying when I ran into one of them. We wept together. One by one, we found each other and were amazed to discover we all were late!"

Nia Davis from Bishop Williams' church was on her way to WTC to have a job interview when it happened. She saw people running and screaming, "Run, run, the building is collapsing!" She had just arrived when the building disappeared in front of her. She was covered with ashes, but she was alive. Had she been earlier as she had planned, she would have been killed.[2]

Two men grabbed a crippled wheelchair-bound woman trapped more than seventy floors above the ground and carried her down to safety. A blind man trapped more than eighty floors above the ground sent his beloved guide dog away from him and an excruciating death. But through the smoke and debris, the heroic dog came back, miraculously leading his master through pitch black smoke, shattered glass, and twisted steel down those many flights to safety.

In October 2001 at our General Conference in Louisville, Kentucky, I sat at a table for ministers' wives with a minister's wife from New York. She told me that she was sick that fateful Tuesday and stayed home. Her daughter worked nearby, but she was delayed. Although many good people perished in that horrible happening, we keep hearing story after story of God's care. On that horrendous day, heroes of hope helped others.

An investment company located in the WTC had 109 employees. They lost 60 of the 109, including two of their top executives. They lost all their records, equipment, desks, computers—everything was gone! They had to put the company back together from memory. One retired official volunteered to come back and help them. Only a few of the survivors elected not to return to the company. Most of them decided to push past disaster, despair, and devastation and rebuild! They held on to hope.

These stories testify of God's goodness in the midst of terror. They help us to hope when all hope seems gone. The eleventh chapter of Hebrews records a long list of heroes of faith and hope. Then in verse 36 the writer simply said, "And others." Their story does not paint a rosy picture of victory, but the writer described them, "Of whom the world was not worthy."

In Matthew 24:2, Jesus told about terror coming upon the Temple and Jerusalem. "And Jesus said unto them, See ye not all these things? verily I say unto you, There shall not be left here one stone upon another, that shall not be thrown down." Destruction did come. Many perished but some survived. Those great heroes of hope carried the hope of this great gospel to the then known world.

Hundreds perished in the WTC. Many American soldiers are losing their lives in Iraq. These are the "And others!" But Lesa Engelthaler, *Dallas Morning News*, said it well, "Hope comes from knowing Who is in control. We have a sovereign, loving God who is in control of every event in our lives." Heroes of hope still preach the gospel of the mighty God in Christ in the Mideast and some still receive it.

In his book, *You Gotta Have the Want-To*, Allan C. Oggs tells that at his birth, he was brain damaged. The doctor said, "He'll never walk, talk or see. My best advice for you is to pray for a merciful death." But that doctor did not know the Oggs' Pentecostal pastor, J. B. Thomas. "Brother Thomas visited the hospital and the home twice a day to pray for us." For several days, the church organized a twenty-four-hour-a-day prayer chain. The baby did not die and was not blind. Although there was little knowledge and less treatment for cerebral palsy in those days, the baby slowly began to improve, grew up and learned to ride a bicycle. "My parents never let me feel sorry for myself, sit in a corner and pout that everything was against me, *nobody loves me, I'll just go eat worms!*"

School challenged him. He sailed through kindergarten, even winning a beauty contest. Despite his poor coordination and poor motor skills, he entered a track meet and tried out for everything. He got a medal for trying which simply said, "Congratulations." In other words, "We admire you and respect you and most of all, we love you."

In his late teens, Oggs found the Lord, went to Bible school and married the prettiest girl there and began his life's work in the ministry. Read his remarkable story . . . the heartwarming, indomitable spirit of a man who has to "stand stiffly placing [his] right arm behind [his] back and grasping it tightly with [his] left to hold it down." After thirty-three years of preaching, he began hesitantly, "But it happened again. Before I had gotten very far into my talk, I felt the anointing of the Holy Spirit wash over me again . . . the Word was becoming flesh again."[3] Brother Oggs lives on hope.

Robert Spooner, art dealer, sells a beautiful embossed scripture from Jeremiah. "I know the plans I have for you, a future and a hope." Although this piece of art is quite expensive, we have had to reorder it several times. I remember one single woman who apparently didn't have a lot of money. "Can I put that on layaway?" she asked.

"Of course," I answered. "Just try to pay it off in about ninety days. Our storage space is so limited." When she made the final payment, she left with a smile, convinced she had a future and a hope.

The Jews wrote scripture on the doorpost, wore it as frontlets, and carried His Word throughout generations. Jesus knew the Word. The apostles quoted it. We must hide it in our hearts.

I remember an old scripture plaque of John 3:16 that hung in my grandmother's home, then later in my mother's home. One day I asked my mother if she would leave that plaque to me. She answered, "Take it now." My oldest daughter now has it, and I hope it survives many more years.

The biblical Book of Job fascinates me. When things get incredibly rough, I like to reread his story. He replied to his "friend," Bildad, "How long will ye vex my soul, and break me in pieces with words?" (Job 19:1). Then in verses 25-26, he said, "For I know that my redeemer liveth, and that he shall stand at the latter day upon the earth: and though after my skin worms destroy this body, yet in my flesh shall I see God." What a triumphant speech in the midst of trials that were completely a mystery to him. Job is a great hero of hope.

Nancy Guthrie in her book, *Holding on to Hope*, said, "Do you find yourself yearning for heaven in the midst of your sorrow or difficulty? Perhaps that is part of the purpose in your pain—a new perspective, a proper perspective, about life on this earth and the life after."

Jesus said, "Let not your heart be troubled: ye believe in God, believe also in me. In my Father's house are many mansions: if it were not so, I would have told you. I go to prepare a place for you. And if I go and prepare a place for you, I will come again, and receive you unto myself: that where I am, there ye may be also" (John 14:1-3). Jesus is building fine homes for heroes of hope. As Dr. James M. Gray said, "Who can mind the journey when the road leads home."

At the holiday season, all roads seem to lead home. One Christmas my husband and I and our first-born two-year-old son battled ice and snow as we crossed Monteagle Mountain, heading home from college. We stopped in a restaurant on top of the mountain to get coffee to keep us awake that dark, stormy night. As we sat there, a trucker came in to use the phone. "I just rolled my truck off the mountain," he said. This added to our concerns. The snow was so thick that J. O. rolled down the window and looked out trying to stay on the road. Late that night weary and tired, we pulled into the old white farmhouse on Robinson Road in Nashville. There stood Papa Wallace in the doorway, arms outstretched to welcome us home. Papa Wallace was a hero of hope to all of us Wallaces!

When we lived in St. Louis after our children were grown, they too drove through ice and snow and bad roads heading home for Christmas. We waited and worried. Then one by one they pulled into the driveway with sleepy children of their own, all glad to be home. The hope of heaven, our eternal home, keeps us going.

Hope and the bright promise of that great celebration, the Marriage Supper of the Lamb, carry us through storms, over mountain roads, down crooked highways through deep valleys of despair. But He'll be waiting, arms outstretched to welcome us home!

We keep on, headed to our eternal home, sowing seeds of hope, but we will reap in joy if we faint not.

If we are at the end of nowhere, we can still choose to be in the Spirit as we open our hearts and lift our hopes to God. We can step into His presence as simply as stepping into a phone booth, closing our eyes to our surroundings and focusing on Him. At home alone, in a crowded room, or on an airplane, just step into His presence.

On a small, nothing island, used as a Roman penal island, the Alcatraz of the Mediterranean, called Patmos, lived an old man probably seventy-five or eighty, John. He was in a nothing place, going nowhere. But John chose to be in the Spirit on the Lord's day.

Suddenly John heard a loud, trumpet-like voice saying, "I am Alpha and Omega, the beginning and the ending." John heard, then he saw. He saw Jesus in all His glory, clothed in white and girded with gold, hair white as snow and eyes like a flame of fire. What a vision of the mighty God in Christ in that nowhere place, just because John was in the Spirit on the Lord's day!

God's message was, "Don't be afraid! I am the First and the Last. I have the keys of death and hell." What a message for an old man who had been boiled in oil, left to die on a forsaken island! Rome could not write the last chapter of John's life. God was the first and the last, the finisher of John's race.

You may feel hopeless. Think you are a nobody in a

godforsaken place, going nowhere. You may think you are at the end, but God has a future and a hope for you. He says, "I know where you are, your down sittings and your uprisings. I am writing the details of your life. I will write the final chapter."

John, the apostle of love, was the youngest of them all. He was very close to Jesus. He saw Jesus feed thousands, heal the sick, raise the dead, but John had never seen Jesus as He was that day. John fell at His feet as though dead, then Jesus laid His hand on John, saying, "Don't be afraid. Circumstances will not write the last chapter of your life. I will write the last chapter of your life."

All the apostles paid the supreme sacrifice for this blessed hope that we enjoy today. Peter wrote that we were begotten unto a living hope by the resurrection of Jesus Christ. We may suffer for a while. Peter and the saints to whom he wrote did indeed suffer, but we can rejoice with joy unspeakable because of that blessed hope.

Most things that are of great value have been purchased through suffering. The fifty-six men who signed the Declaration of Independence were not wild-eyed, rabble-rousing ruffians, but soft-spoken educated men. What a price they paid for the hope of liberty! Five were tortured as traitors. Twelve had their homes burned. Two lost sons who served with General George Washington. Another had two sons captured by the British Navy. Another had to move his family constantly while he served in Congress without pay. Soldiers or vandals looted the properties of Clymer, Ellery, Gwinnet, Heyward, Rutledge and Walton and Middleton. While John Hart's wife lay dying, he was driven from her bedside and his thirteen children fled for their lives. Morris and Livingston suffered similiar fates.

When the British General Cornwallis commandeered the Thomas Nelson Jr. home, Nelson quietly urged General Washington to open fire, destroying the home. Nelson died bankrupt. The home of Francis Lewis was destroyed, his wife jailed where she soon died. These men gave their all for their hope of a free country. We enjoy the glory in our great Independence Day celebrations, but suffering came first—then glory. These patriots were great heroes of hope.

The Tennessean carried a story about a Christian family from Africa who escaped from a Muslim dominated country with its persecution. They made their way to America and with the help of a local church were just about ready to move into a little home of their own. Then the father fell sick and died, but the mother still has hope. She believes that here her children can get an education and have a future and a hope.

The story of David Rothenberg made the newspapers a few years ago. What a tragic story of a father who, in a fit of rage, went into his son's room, poured kerosene all over the room, all over the little boy, then set him on fire. Somehow David lived through it, though ninety-five percent of his body was covered with third-degree burns. To this day, he has virtually no skin. It is estimated that David will have approximately five thousand operations in his lifetime. Each year they have to open him up so that he can grow. Along with a few saints and poets, David Rothenberg is aware of the greatest miracle of all: LIFE ITSELF. At the age of seven, he had the audacity to say:

I am alive!
I am alive!

I am alive!
I didn't miss out on living!
And that is wonderful enough for me!

Someone has said, "Growing old is not for sissies!" George Frederic Handel was an old fogy, but when he was a young man, he was the talk of England, the best-paid composer on earth. His fame soared around the world.

But the glory passed, audiences dwindled, and one project after another failed. Handel grew depressed. The stress brought on a case of palsy that crippled some of his fingers. "Handel's great days are over," wrote Frederick the Great, "his inspiration is exhausted."

Yet Handel's troubles also matured him, and his music became more heartfelt. One morning Handel received a collection of various biblical texts from Charles Jennens. The opening words from Isaiah 40 moved Handel: *Comfort ye my people.*

On August 22, 1741, he began composing music for the words. Twenty-three days later, the world had *Messiah*, which opened in London to enormous crowds on March 23, 1743. Handel led from his harpsichord. King George II, who was present that night, surprised everyone by leaping to his feet during the "Hallelujah Chorus." From that day, audiences everywhere have stood in reverence during the stirring words: *Hallelujah! And He shall reign forever and ever!*[4] The "Hallelujah Chorus" is a song for heroes of hope.

A thirty-minute brawl with a mountain lion gave Andy Peterson his first glimpse of God. At twenty-one, he moved from his Minnesota home to Colorado with no plans for school or a job. A drug addiction started at age eleven worsened. He declared bankruptcy three times. His dad was a believer, but Andy said, "Religion didn't make sense."

He got a job as a park ranger at Lakewood State Park. On April 30, 1998, he started on his weekly hike at neighboring Roxborough State Park in Englewood, Colorado, armed only with a Swiss Army knife.

During his descent from Carpenter's Peak, a 100-pound mountain lion attacked the 130-pound twenty-four-year-old. He stunned the animal by stabbing it with the two-inch blade of his knife and jabbing his thumb in its eye. "Three things flashed through my mind and gave me an adrenaline boost: friends, family, and how I'd be remembered, which I knew was not in the best light."

As he neared the last mile of the trail, Peterson looked behind his shoulder and saw the lion eyeing him from a tree. "I turned around again, and instead of the cat, I saw the transparent face of Jesus. The fear was gone and an overwhelming peace engulfed me."

Bleeding badly Peterson was airlifted to a hospital where he endured six hours of surgery resulting in seventy staples to close the twenty inches of bite marks in his head.

"My dad came and told me about Jesus and on that day I got one foot on God's path." Andy now lives in Murfreesboro near Nashville. He lets his light shine by selling supplies to Christian bookstores. That was how I met him. He told me about the lion attacking him. The January/February 2003 issue of *New Man* magazine carried his amazing story. The media covered bits and pieces of the amazing story but only Oprah Winfrey and a Colorado TV station permitted him to mention Jesus' name on their programs.

We survive dark, desperate disasters with God's help, then give Him the glory as we reap the harvest of hope. Even a puny crop will yield some seed for the next harvest. I transplanted some of my mother's peonies to St. Louis about fifteen years ago. When we moved to Columbus, Mississippi, we took them along with a climbing rose from Grandfather Wallace's house over twenty years ago. The flowers were moved to Nashville, but the peonies were planted in a place with not much sunshine. Their tiny shoots were coming up valiantly so my husband transplanted them to a sunnier spot. We have had several blooms this year. Peonies need some sunshine, and we need God's sunshine and hope. Things happen—sometimes disaster—but there is always something left. God writes the final chapter concerning His heroes of hope!

CHAPTER 13

The Joy of Finding Hope

"He who laughs, lasts."[1] Attitude means so much in every situation. C. S. Lewis said, "Joy is the serious business of heaven."

In Acts 20:22-24, Paul wrote: "And now, behold, I go bound in the spirit unto Jerusalem, not knowing the things that shall befall me there: save that the Holy Ghost witnesseth in every city, saying that bonds and afflictions abide me. But none of these things move me, neither count I my life dear unto myself, so that I might finish my course with *joy*" (italics added).

In II Corinthians 11:23-28, Paul listed his many problems: "In stripes above measure, in prisons more frequent, in deaths oft. Of the Jews five times received I forty stripes save one. Thrice was I beaten with rods, once was I stoned, thrice I suffered shipwreck, a night and a day I have been in the deep; in journeyings often, in perils of waters, in perils of robbers, in perils by mine own countrymen, in perils by the heathen, in perils in the city, in perils in the wilderness, in perils in the sea, in perils among false brethren; in weariness and painfulness, in watchings often, in hunger and thirst, in fastings often, in cold and nakedness. Beside those things that are without, that which cometh upon me daily, the care of all the churches." Yet Paul said, "I will *glory* of the things which concern mine infirmities" (italics added) (II Corinthians 11:30). Paul had indeed been there and done that. In Philippians 3:8, he said, "I count all things but loss for the excellency of the knowledge of Christ Jesus." In II Corinthians 4:17, he called his troubles "our light affliction, which is but for a moment." And he is right. In the light of eternity, any problems we have here during our allotted "three score and ten" are very light—just for a moment.

In James 1:2, that apostle of Jerusalem said, "My brethren, count it all *joy* when ye fall into divers temptations" (italics added).

Brother Michael Rickenbakker said that in all the scriptures about the apostles, we find no record of them asking for physical healing or financial prosperity. They asked only for boldness in preaching the gospel to all the world. They found joy in spreading the good news.

Habakkuk 3:17-19 sums it all up: "Although the fig tree shall not blossom, neither shall fruit be in the vines; the labour of the olive shall fail, and the fields shall yield no meat; the flock shall be cut off from the fold, and there shall be no herd in the stalls: yet I will rejoice in the LORD, I will joy in the God of my salvation. The LORD God is my strength, and he will make my feet like hinds' feet, and he will make me to walk upon mine high places." In our success driven society, Habakkuk would probably be classified as an utter failure; yet Habakkuk took joy in his salvation.

According to Samuel W. Shoemaker, "The surest mark of a Christian is not faith or even love, but *joy.*" Another writer called faith a force not a farce. David predicted that, "Joy cometh in the morning" (Psalm 30:5). Happiness comes from the same root as happening, suggesting that happiness is based on something happening to us—something circumstantial, a feeling! Joy is a choice, an attitude. We can avoid joy. We can whine. We can grow bitter. Barbara Johnson learned that. She said, "Pain is inevitable but misery is optional." We cannot avoid pain, but we can avoid joy.

The *USA WEEKEND* magazine of March 7-9, 2003, carried an article titled "The Happiest Guy." The article said, "People actually can condition themselves for genuine happiness . . . Truly happy people are able to, for example, recall special moments and use them as psychological tools to deal with adversity."

Old-time testimonies used to do that when people would recall how God had blessed them on many different occasions. Paul mentioned in II Timothy 1:5: "When I call to remembrance the unfeigned faith that is in thee, which dwelt first in thy grandmother Lois, and thy mother Eunice; and I am persuaded that in thee also."

Remember the happy times. Forget the bad times. Philippians 3:13-14, "Forgetting those things (all those troubles and trials) which are behind, and reaching forth unto those things which are before, I press toward the mark for the prize of the high calling of God in Christ Jesus" (parentheses added).

The article also mentioned how that happy people had "signature strengths"—such as a sense of humor or the capacity to love—and learned how to use them every day, in all kinds of situations. They often ended up the happiest of all. Don't you like to hang out with happy people? Avoid negative, bitter whiners.

Paul said in Philippians 4:8, "Finally, brethren, whatsoever things are true, whatsoever things are honest, whatsoever things are just, whatsoever things are pure, whatsoever things are lovely, whatsoever things are of good report; if there be any virtue, and if there be any praise, think on these things." Then he assured us in the nineteenth verse, "But my God shall supply all your need according to his riches in glory by Christ Jesus." That should start us singing the "Hallelujah Chorus!"

One writer said, "Most people are about as happy as they make up their minds to be." A children's chorus also encourages us to be happy:

The time to be happy is now,
The place to be happy is here,
The way to be happy is to make others happy.
So let's spread a little happiness down here.

(Author unknown)

I remember Brother Bobo in our small Finley church. For years he was the only man who attended regularly. His testimony was always, "I thank the Lord for food, raiment, and shelter." (As a child, I wondered, "Who in the world was Raymond?") A sharecropper, Brother Bobo lived in a small farmhouse with his wife and several children. A kind, gentle man with no complaints or tales of hardship. After I married and moved away, I lost track of the family. Isaiah 29:19 refers to people like Brother Bobo. "The meek shall increase their joy." There is a pew in the beautiful new Finley Pentecostal church dedicated to that faithful man.

Deep sorrow often precedes joy. Barbara Johnson shed many a tear over her sons. One was killed in Vietnam, another in a terrible car wreck. Then a third son came out of the closet to declare that he was gay. For a year Barbara was in the depths of depression and toyed with the idea of suicide. Finally she turned to her Lord and His Word. Now she writes inspirational books with a great sense of humor. Her first one was *Where Does a Mother Go to Resign.* Later she wrote others. *Stick a Geranium in Your Hat and Be Happy* was the last one that I have read. Her faith and tremendous sense of humor have helped many a woman to find some sort of joy in difficult times. "The joy of the LORD is your strength" (Nehemiah 8:10). As Job found out, sorrow can be turned into joy. (See Job 41:22.)

One of the special rewards for those who pray at the altar with sinners is the radiant look of glory that shines on the face of a repentant person as he feels the load of sin roll off his back. David said in Psalm 51:12: "Restore unto me the joy of thy salvation."

Dale Carnegie said, "It isn't what you have, or who you are or what you are doing that makes you happy or unhappy. It is what you think about." We need to guard the mind and remember to think on "whatsoever things are pure." Another writer said, "There is only one happiness in life—to love and be loved." Og Mandino said, "Without enthusiasm you are chained to a life of mediocrity, but with it you can accomplish miracles." Mary Kay Ash, successful businesswoman, said, "If you think you can, you can. If you think you can't, you're right." Many women who follow her philosophy are driving pink Cadillacs.

In his inimitable style, Will Rogers said, "So live that you wouldn't be ashamed to sell the family parrot to the town gossip!"

Go to the Word and listen to Paul in I Thessalonians 5:16-18: "Rejoice evermore. Pray without ceasing. In every thing give thanks: for this is the will of God in Christ Jesus concerning you." In his book, *You Gotta Keep Dancin'*, Tim Hansel had to face the fact that he would be in pain for the rest of his life. "It wasn't the pain that was thwarting me as much as it was my *attitude* toward the pain. I realized that though the difficulties were undeniably real, and would remain so for the rest of my life, I had the opportunity to *choose* a new freedom and joy if I wanted to."[2]

My own problems with my back are not nearly so severe as Hansel's, but I too have learned to accept the pain and keep moving on. One thing I can do is use my computer for an hour or so at a time. I thank God for my quad cane and my husband's strong right arm.

Confined to a wheelchair as a young woman, Ruby Martin taught Bible school at Jackson College of Ministries until she was past eighty. Allan Oggs wrote about it this way, "*You Gotta Have the Want-To.*"

During the difficult days of the Great Depression, we sang heartily about "Joy Unspeakable and Full of Glory" and "There Is Sunshine in My Soul Today." Hope brought music to our lives. When Japan bombed Pearl Harbor, Kate Smith lifted our hopes when she sang "God Bless America."

God has truly blessed America. Since winning World War II, America has prospered amazingly. His blessings flow like a river of life. Prosperity sometimes leads us to too much self-confidence. We are prone to forget the God who gave victory and "daily loadeth us with benefits" (Psalm 68:19). His river of life refreshes us and gives the thirsty life.

There's a wonderful story from the life of Lawrence of Arabia that illustrates this. When Lawrence took some Arabian chieftains to Paris for the Paris Peace Conference, they were astounded by the conveniences of the city. What they found most amazing of all was the running water that flowed from the faucets in their hotel rooms. Life in the desert had taught them the scarcity and the value of water. But now by simply turning on the faucet, they could have all the water they wanted. They drank it, bathed in it, and still there was more.

"When it came time for Lawrence and his party to check out of their hotel rooms, the manager found the Arab chieftains doing a curious thing. They were trying to detach the faucets so they could take them with them to the desert. He tried to explain that the faucets were useless without being connected to the pipes which were in turn attached to the water mains leading to the city's reservoirs."[3]

Old-time Pentecostal preachers said it well, "You've got to get under the spout where the glory comes out." It is not our wisdom, our talent, or our ability that gives us hope for the future. It is His amazing grace. We can allow His river of life-giving water to flow through our lives like a pipeline to bless others. If we become dependent on self and never give out, we will become like a small self-filled, silt-clogged muddy puddle, not even as impressive as the Dead Sea with no outlet and in which nothing lives.

Don't let your pipeline to glory get clogged. Keep the river of joy flowing! Remember to sing, "Great Is Thy Faithfulness." "It is of the LORD's mercies that we are not consumed, because his compassions fail not. They are new every morning: great is thy faithfulness." I also love to sing the song, "Jesus, I'll never forget what You've done for me. Jesus, I'll never forget how You set me free."

Two parables in Matthew 13:44-45 tell us about a hidden treasure. A man, probably an ordinary farmer, felt his plow hit what he thought was a rock. Imagine his shock to discover a treasure. A treasure so priceless that he joyfully sold all he had and bought the field. The world is the field. Jesus gave His all to purchase the treasure (the church) hidden amongst the dirt of this world. In just thirty-four words, Jesus told the next parable of the pearl of great price. A priceless pearl of such great beauty that the merchant (again a type of Christ) sold all he had to buy that pearl—the church.

What joy floods our souls as we try to comprehend the great love Christ has for the church, for us who are part of the body of Christ. We are the treasure that Jesus came to seek and to save. No wonder we rejoice as our finite minds try to comprehend His great love for us. Let your joybells ring victoriously. He has conquered death, hell, and the grave! We are His treasure, hidden in the world, in it but not of it. What a hope!

In Galatians 5:22-23, Paul listed the fruit of the Spirit. He listed joy as the second fruit, placed right between love and peace. Perhaps it is joy that holds love and peace together. When we begin to grasp the place that joy fills in our lives, we can begin to comprehend that our troubles and trials, our cross is not a drudgery but can become a joy, a delight.

Oh, it is true that joy is free, but it is not cheap. He bought us with a price and we pay a price as we follow Him. But He considers us a "pearl of great price, a hidden treasure." When that sinks into our minds, then we can "count it all joy."

Remember Jesus had a hard time teaching the apostles. He called the two Emmaus disciples, "O fools, and slow of heart to believe all that the prophets have spoken: Ought not Christ to have suffered these things, and to enter into his glory? And beginning at Moses and all the prophets, he expounded unto them in all the scriptures the things concerning himself" (Luke 24:25-27).

Then He had to deal even more explicitly with Thomas, who seemed determined not to believe. "Except I shall see in his hands the print of the nails, and put my finger into the print of the nails, and thrust my hand into his side, I will not believe" (John 20:25). Jesus said to him, "Reach hither thy finger, and behold my hands; and reach hither thy hand, and thrust it into my side: and be not faithless, but believing" (John 20:27).

Some Christians seem determined not to be happy, not to live in hope and joy. But happiness really is a choice. David said, "They that sow in tears shall reap in joy." Solomon cautioned us not to withhold our hearts from joy. (See Ecclesiastes 2:10.) "Eat thy bread with joy"

(Ecclesiastes 9:7). Isaiah added drink to the bread and said, "With joy shall ye draw water" (Isaiah 12:3).

My dear friend, Barbara Washburn, suffered through several trials recently. She wrote the following article, "It's Your Choice!" which she shared with me and gave me permission to use in this book.

"After the Israelites were all settled in Canaan, Joshua gave his farewell address. He admonished the elders to serve the Lord in sincerity and truth and not to worship strange gods like the heathen nations. Then he said those famous words, 'Choose you this day whom ye will serve' (Joshua 24:15).

"One of the sure facts of life is that you will pay for the choices you make. If you make good choices, you will reap the benefits, and if you make bad choices, you will suffer the consequences. One of the greatest choices you'll ever make is whether you will obey the plan of salvation and live for the Lord or reject Him. If you choose to live for Him, He has promised that He will never leave or forsake thee (Hebrews 13:5).

"The second week of January 2000, I got the worst case of flu I have ever had. Even though I worked every day, I felt terrible. It was no ordinary flu. It lasted three weeks, and after I got over it, there were some side effects that lasted for about three months. How many people have you known who died with the flu?

"February 10, 2000, was Thursday. Pay day. After work, I had to go to the bank, to the hospital for a test, the grocery store, K-Mart, and Big Lots. I was getting ready for a retirement dinner at work the next day and I had to get a birthday present. As I came out of Big Lots, it was already 7:00. I was in a hurry to get home. I put my bag in the van on the passenger side and ran around to get in on the driver's side. Suddenly a man stepped up in my face and said, 'This is a robbery or a murder, and it doesn't make any difference to me which!'

"He snatched my purse off my arm and threw it in his truck, spit at me and stuck his tongue out at me with his face snarled up. Then he got in his truck and left. Needless to say, I was very upset, but it wasn't the worst thing that could have happened. How many people have you heard about in the last few years who were robbed and killed?

"One Saturday morning in March, I woke up about 3 A.M. with a terrible pain in my side. It was so severe that I could hardly move. Very slowly I managed to turn over and sit up. I went to the living room and sat on the couch praying, 'Lord, please make this pain go away. I can't stand it!'

"A few minutes later, the pain eased enough that I went back to sleep. When I awoke about 5:30, the pain was gone, but it didn't stay gone. It kept coming and going. About five days later, it finally dawned on me that it was probably pneumonia and wouldn't go away until I went to the doctor and got some medicine. Looking at the X-ray, Dr. Coleman said, 'I see bronchitis right there, asthma right there, and pneumonia right there.'

"He gave me a prescription for some strong medicine that made me sicker than I was. My sister called him about my problem, and he said, 'Go to the emergency room.' Reluctantly I went. They said the medicine the doctor gave me was too strong, so they were going to give me a GI cocktail (mixture of medicines to soothe my stomach.) Any Pentecostal knows better than to drink a cocktail, but I did it.

"Isn't it just like Satan to tell you to go ahead and drink it; it will make you feel better. Don't believe it! For the next three days, my pain was just like that of a woman in labor. When the effects of the cocktail wore off, the pneumonia was gone. Again I ask, 'How many people have you ever known who died of pneumonia?'

"Since I had enjoyed good health all of my life, I was trying to ignore the fact that I might have a serious problem. I had something going on in my stomach that I could not explain. It would get better, then worse, then better, then worse again. The day after Easter, I went to work, but I hurt so badly that I could hardly walk. I made up my mind that as soon as I got off work, I was going straight to the doctor. When I got there, he had already gone. The next morning, I was at his office as soon as they opened. The pain was so strong that I felt almost paralyzed.

"After a short examination, the doctor said, 'What do you think about me putting you in the hospital and running some tests?'

"'Do it,' I said.

"Then he said, 'I'm going to get another doctor to come in and help me look at the tests and see what we can find.'

"That afternoon they did a CT scan and the problem showed up loud and clear. It was a large tumor wrapped around my right ovary. When the doctors explained the problem to me, they said they wouldn't know if it was cancer until they operated. Surgery was scheduled for 6:30 the next morning. After the surgery, Dr. Gregory, the surgeon, said it was cancer, but he got all of it. Then Dr. Greco, one of the best oncologists in Tennessee, was called in to see me. He said I needed a few chemotherapy treatments in case there were still a few cancer cells floating around that might cause trouble later. I was fortunate because the kind of cancer I had was easy to treat. Now, how many people have you ever known who died with cancer?

"My first chemo treatment was scheduled for May 12. They were going to give me two new drugs that had proven to be effective: taxol and carboplatin. They started the treatment with something to keep me from getting sick. Then they started the taxol, the strong medicine. About fifteen or twenty minutes later, I felt something building up inside of me like I was going to explode. My husband noticed my face getting red and came over to see if I was all right. A nurse saw him standing over me and came to me asking, 'How do you feel?'

"I could not explain how I felt. She checked my blood pressure and said, 'It's high.' Then she unhooked the IV. I sure was glad! There's no telling what would have happened if she hadn't. She gave me something to relax me and then they finished the treatment.

"Suppose the man in the parking lot on February 10 had killed me and my body was taken to the funeral home. The man who embalmed me would have probably told the undertaker that my lungs were full of pneumonia and my stomach was full of cancer so I wasn't going to live long anyway. If the pneumonia didn't kill me, the cancer would. Really, that man did me a favor by putting me out of my misery, so I wouldn't have to suffer. But, as it turned out, I survived it all! I give all the glory to Jesus, who paid the price for our healing and to the fact that I made a choice. When I was presented with the gospel of salvation and the benefit package that goes with it, I wholeheartedly accepted. I don't mean to suggest that I am any better than anyone else and Jesus certainly does not owe me anything, but when you obey His plan, the blessings will flow.

"You can also take a step further and join a great church. Then when you are down, you have the prayers and support of a great group of people to help you through it. While I was sick, I talked to a couple of other people who were also sick, but their situation was so much worse than mine because they didn't have a church family as I did.

"Today I am completely healed, and I'm thankful for all the miracles that I have received, but I have learned not to rejoice over miracles. In Luke 10:20, Jesus told His disciples not to rejoice that spirits are subject unto you, but rather rejoice that your name is written in heaven. Miracles were no big deal to Jesus; He just spoke the Word and it was done. But He couldn't just speak a word and provide a way of salvation. It cost Him a lot of pain, rejection, humiliation, and even His life. That's why I appreciate the blessings, but I cherish my salvation."

Yes, salvation is free, but not cheap. Whosoever will may find hope and joy when they turn to Him. True joy is not found at the end of the rainbow. Many scramble up the ladder of success only to find no cup of joy at the top. Faithfulness, endurance, even sorrow are the coins with which to buy true joy. One writer said that our cup of joy is related to the depth of our cup of sorrow. I repeat, joy is free but not cheap.

Acts 16:25 tells the story of Paul and Silas, beaten, then thrown into jail, but at midnight they prayed and sang praises unto God so joyfully that the prisoners heard them. Suddenly an earthquake shook the prison to its foundations. Locked doors swung wide and everyone's bands were loosed. The keeper of the prison was not joyous. He lost all hope and considered suicide. But Paul cried with a loud voice, "Do thyself no harm: for we are all here." A little bit of joyful singing can start a revival. Let it begin in me, Lord. Job 35:10 reminds us that God can give us all songs in the night.

Sometimes we have to risk leaving a comfortable nest and launching into the unknown to find room to spread one's wings. Secretary of State Colin Powell in his biography told that his parents left Jamaica to find work in New York, thus giving him an opportunity for a better education and hope for the future.

I was the first one of my immediate family to leave our small hometown of Finley, Tennessee. I left for California to marry my soldier sweetheart in 1942. I have really never looked back. Mom and Dad moved to Nashville in 1945 partly so that she could play the piano in Papa Wallace's church. Dad knew his job opportunities were better here. My younger brothers and sister all grew up here and chose to stay in the city.

Papa Wallace also broke free from the security of a good job in the Bemis Cotton Mill and pastoring the Bemis Pentecostal Church. Past age fifty, he felt the call to go east of the Tennessee River to establish more churches. All of his family except a married son, Cleatus, went with him and found new jobs and new opportunities in a wider field. Happiness and great joy may lie for you just beyond your security box, especially if God is calling you to wider service.

All opportunities for joy in serving are not limited to the young and adventurous. The retired and aged do not have to surrender to hopelessness, apathy, and laziness. Youth is renewed when we set goals and make commitments. Energy is generated. Enthusiasm and creativity are generated when you decide to live rather than die. Look up! Face the sun of service, and the shadow of depression and doubt will fall behind you.

The Tennessean recently carried the story of a one-hundred-year-old woman who found happiness in playing an organ in a nursing home. Like Paul in Acts 20:24, she is finishing her course with joy. Praise and worship bring hope and joy to the aged as well as to the young children singing, "Jesus Loves Me."

Jimmy Carter's mother, a registered nurse, left her small hometown of Plainsville, Georgia, and went to India to serve there. That was not a peanut challenge!

We have served for short terms in India. I well remember our last visit there; we were met at about midnight by natives shouting, "Go home, Yankees!" What a joy it was to see the familiar faces of the local pastors. Surely, He is "the joy of the whole earth" (Psalm 48:2).

Joy and victory can shine in the most adverse circumstances. When Scott Graham spoke at the Tennessee camp meeting, he related the following story. A preacher friend of his sat by a stranger on an airplane. The man asked the usual questions, "What is your name? Where are you from? And what do you do?" The minister told him that he pastored a United Pentecostal church in that city. The stranger's response caused him to ask, "Have you ever attended a Pentecostal church?" "No, we hardly ever went to church," was his reply. Then he told him that he was a prisoner of war in the "Hanoi Hilton" in North Vietnam.

"I was caged in a wire cage too small to stand up in or lie down. We were beaten, fed barely enough watery soup to survive and tortured in ways beyond description. Every night after the guards had gone some distance away, this one fellow prisoner began to softly sing:

O victory in Jesus, my Savior, forever,
He sought me and bought me with His redeem-
ing blood;
He loved me ere I knew Him and all my love is
due Him,
He plunged me to victory, beneath the cleansing
flood.

(E. M. Bartlett)

"Every night he sang that song about victory. I found out that he attended a United Pentecostal church. I never did get to see him. I don't even know his name. We called him 'Victory.' What a man!"

Satan could not steal that unknown soldier's victory in one of the worst prisons known to man. His song in the nighttime brought hope to all the prisoners, and his story will perhaps bring hope into others' dark night of the soul. Our hope in Him is truly joy unspeakable and full of glory—true victory!

Everyone wants joy, even Jesus, "for the joy that was set before him endured the cross, despising the shame, and is set down at the right hand of the throne of God" (Hebrews 12:2).

Natural joy is not a fruit of the Spirit. We find the fruit

of spiritual joy as a result of receiving the Holy Ghost and walking in the Spirit. Natural joy does not last. The worldly man is never satisfied. Some deliberately seek joy in a bottle to drown sorrow. "Let us eat, drink and be merry for tomorrow we die," is their philosophy. Solomon spoke of the laughter of the fool and called it vanity. (See Ecclesiastes 7:6, also 11:9.) Despite his riches and success, to Solomon all seemed vanity. His conclusion was for us to "fear God, and keep his commandments."

On the other hand, the spiritual man finds the joy of the Holy Spirit to be an overflowing well of hope and joy. The Philippian jailor, the Ethiopian eunuch, and the merchant who found the pearl of great price all found true hope and joy.

In the midst of great trouble, Habakkuk found strength and joy in the God of his salvation (Habakkuk 3:16-19). Paul and Barnabus found great joy in serving others. (See Acts 15:3.) At midnight in jail, Paul and Silas prayed and sang praises until the place shook (Acts 16:25-35).

During the days of the Great Depression as a child, I found security in listening to my Grandmother Weedman singing, "Jesus is all the world to me, my life, my joy, my all; He is my strength from day to day, without Him I would fall."

My hope is in Him!

Recommended Reading List

Adam, Henri Nouwen, Orbis Books, Maryknoll, NY, 1997

Be Hopeful, Warren Wiersbe, Victor Books, Wheaton, IL, 1982

Couples in the Bible, Sylvia Charles, Hensley Pub, Tulsa, OK, 1998

Forge of Faith: No Stranger to Death, Jerra K. Gadd with Peggy L. Jenkins, PegLee Publishers, Brownsburg, IN, 2003

Future and a Hope, A, Lloyd Ogilvie, Word Publishing, Dallas, 1988

Head First: The Biology of Hope and the Healing Power of the Human Spirit, Norman Cousins, E. P. Dutton, NY, 1989

Heart of America, The, Mike Trout, Zondervan Publishing, Grand Rapids, MI, 1998

Holding on to Hope, Nancy Guthrie, Tyndale House Publishing, Inc., Wheaton, IL, 2002

Hope Again, Charles Swindoll, Word Publishing, Dallas, TX, 1996

Hope, Helping One Succeed, Word Aflame Publications, Hazelwood, MO, 2002

If It's Going to Be, It's Up to Me, Robert Schuller, Harper, San Francisco, CA, 1997

I've Got a Secret, Kimberlee Stone, Armor Books, Lawerenceville, GA, 2002

Lost in Church, Jonathan R. Cash, Whitaker House, New Kensington, PA, 2002

Miracle of Hope, The, Charles Allen, Fleming Revell, Old Tappan, NJ, 1973

Pack Up Your Gloomees in a Great Big Box, Barbara Johnson, Word Pub., Dallas, 1993

Purpose Driven Life, The, Rick Warren, Zondervan, Grand Rapids, MI, 2002

Sustaining Power of Hope, The, Leslie B. Flynn, Scripture Press Publications, Wheaton, IL, 1985

Tell Your Heart to Beat Again, Dutch Sheets, Regal Books, Gospel Light, CA, 2002

Turning Hurts into Halos, Robert Schuller, Thomas Nelson Publishers, Nashville, TN, 2000

Ultimate Success, David Shibley, New Leaf Press, Green Forest, AR, 1993

You Gotta Have the Want-To, Allan C. Oggs, Pulpit Ministries, Metairie, LA, 1987

You Gotta Keep Dancin', Tim Hansel, Chariot Victor Publishing, Colorado, CO, 1985

Notes

Chapter 1

[1]Charles Allen, *The Miracle of Hope* (Old Tappan, NJ: Fleming Revell Co., 1973), 23.

[2]"Why Can't I Deal with Depression?" *Christianity Today*, 1982.

[3]Leslie B. Flynn, *The Sustaining Power of Hope* (Wheaton, IL: Victor Books, 1985), 11.

[4]Lloyd Ogilvie, *A Future and a Hope*, (Dallas: Word Publishing, 1988), 41.

Chapter 2

[1]David Shibley, *Ultimate Success* (Green Forest, AR: New Leaf Press, 1993), 50.

[2]Norman Cousins, *Head First: The Biology of Hope and the Healing Power of the Human Spirit* (New York: E. P. Dutton, 1989), 98.

[3]Dutch Sheets, *Tell Your Heart to Beat Again: Discover the Good in What You're Going Through* (Ventura, CA: Gospel Light Publications, 2002), 27.

[4]Ibid, back cover of the book.

[5]Tim Hansel, *You Gotta Keep Dancin'* (Colorado Springs: Chariot Victor Publishing, 1985), 15.

[6]Lloyd Ogilvie, *A Future and a Hope* (Dallas: Word Publishing, 1988), 64.

Chapter 3

[1]Charles Allen, *The Miracle of Hope* (Old Tappan, NJ: Fleming Revell Co., 1973), 11.

[2]Thomas M. Freiling, Editor, *George W. Bush on God and Country* (Fairfax, VA: Allegiance Press, 2004), 4.

[3]Lloyd Ogilvie, *A Future and a Hope* (Dallas: Word Publishing, 1988), 34.

[4]Nancy Guthrie, *Holding on to Hope*, (Wheaton, IL: Tyndale House Publishing, Inc., 2002), 40.

[5]Lloyd Ogilvie, *A Future and a Hope* (Dallas: Word Publishing, 1988), 35.

Chapter 4
[1]December 2002 issue of *Ladies' Home Journal.*

Chapter 5
[1]Charles Allen, *The Miracle of Hope* (Old Tappan, NJ: Fleming Revell Co., 1973), 49.

[2]Tim Hansel, *You Gotta Keep Dancin'* (Colorado Springs: Chariot Victor Publishing, 1985), 36- 37.

Chapter 6
[1]Franklin Graham, *Rebel with a Cause* (Nashville: Thomas Nelson, Inc., 1995), 297.

[2]Judith S. Wallerstein & Sandra Blakeslee, *Second Chances* (Boston: Houghton Mifflin Company, 1989), xi.

Chapter 7
[1]Sylvia Charles, *Couples in the Bible* (Tulsa, OK: Hensley Publishing, 1998), 35.

[2]Charles Allen, *The Miracle of Hope* (Old Tappan, NJ: Fleming Revell Co., 1973), 17.

[3]*Hymns of Faith and Inspiration* (Nashville, TN: Ideals, a division of Guideposts, 1990), 20-21.

[4]Tim Hansel, *You Gotta Keep Dancin'* (Colorado Springs: Chariot Victor Publishers, 1985), 99-100.

[5]Barbara Johnson, *Pack Up Your Gloomees in a Great Big Box* (Dallas: Word Publishing, 1993), 1.

Chapter 8
[1]"The Science of Happiness," *Newsweek Magazine* (10 September 2002).

[2]Tim Hansel, *You Gotta Keep Dancin'* (Colorado Springs: Chariot Victor Publishing, 1985), 66.

[3]Norman Cousins, *Anatomy of an Illness* (New York: William Norton and Co., 1979), 86.

[4]Tim Hansel, *You Gotta Keep Dancin'* (Colorado Springs: Chariot Victor Publishing, 1985), 68.

[5]Barbara Johnson, *Pack Up Your Gloomees in a Great Big Box* (Dallas: Word Publishing, 1993), 21.

Chapter 9

[1]Jerra K. Gadd with Peggy L. Jenkins, *Forge of Faith: No Stranger to Death* (Brownsburg, IN: PegLee Publishers, 2003), xi-xii.

[2]Lloyd Ogilvie, *A Future and a Hope* (Dallas: Word Publishing, 1988), 63.

[3]Warren Wiersbe, *Be Hopeful* (Wheaton, IL: Victor Books, 1982), 8.

Chapter 10

[1]Warren Wiersbe, *Be Hopeful* (Wheaton, IL: Victor Books, 1982), 25.

Chapter 11

[1]Robert H. Schuller, *If It's Going to Be, It's Up to Me* (San Francisco, CA: Harper Collins Publishers, 1997), 175.

[2]Robert H. Schuller, *Turning Hurts into Halos* (Nashville, TN: Thomas Nelson, Inc, 2000), 34.

Chapter 12

[1]Nancy Guthrie, *Holding on to Hope* (Wheaton, IL: Tyndale House Publishing, Inc., 2002), vii.

[2]*End-Time Handmaidens & Servants Magazine*, May 2002. Used by permission.

[3]Allan Oggs, *You Gotta Have the Want-To* (Kenner, LA: Pulpit Ministries, 1987), 9, 14.

[4]Robert J. Morgan, *Real Stories for the Soul* (Nashville, TN: Thomas Nelson, Inc., 2000), 53-55.

Chapter 13

[1]John Bartlett, *Familiar Quotations, Sixteenth Edition* (Boston: Little, Brown and Company, 1992), 288.

[2]Tim Hansel, *You Gotta Keep Dancin'* (Colorado Springs: Chariot Victor Publishing, 1985), 48.

[3]Lloyd Ogilvie, *A Future and a Hope,* (Dallas: Word Publishing, 1988), 197.

J. O. and Mary Wallace

About the Author

MARY HARDWICK WALLACE grew up in the small town of Finley, Tennessee, the eldest of four siblings. In about 1919 some pioneer Pentecostal preachers brought the message of Pentecost to West Tennessee and Wallace's grandmother and mother gladly received it. Even though she grew up during the Great Depression years, those years, in her eyes, were far from impoverished. She loved music, writing, speech and especially her church.

In 1942 she married her soldier sweetheart, James Onell Wallace, and with his father, J. W. Wallace, they helped pioneer the West Nashville Pentecostal Church. While J. O. was still in the military, they founded the Goodlettsville Pentecostal Church and later the Woodbine Pentecostal Church. They also founded West Nashville Kindergarten/Nursery School (now Knob Hill Child Care Center). While teaching kindergarten Wallace began writing kindergarten Sunday school curricula. Later she joined the team who pioneered Word Aflame Sunday School Curriculum and served with them for twenty-seven years. For twelve years she served as editor for the Pentecostal Publishing House.

She has written and compiled eighteen books in addition to curricula, numerous Bible stories and articles. She has taught Sunday school seminars and owned her own Christian bookstore. The Wallaces think that their six children, twelve grandchildren, and one great granddaughter are God's greatest gift to them.